The Red Heart

BOOK 1 IN THE RED CENTRE SERIES

EMILY HUSSEY

WINSOME BOOKS

Copyright © 2018 Emily Hussey

ISBN 978-0-648297208

Editor: Lauren Clarke

Cover Design: Getcovers

Images: Depositphotos

Published by Winsome Books 2018

2nd Edition October 2023

A division of Winsome Enterprises Pty Ltd

Adelaide, South Australia

Contents

ALSO BY EMILY HUSSEY

The Red Centre Series
Journey to the Heart
The Red Heart
Trust Your Heart
Follow Your Heart

Stand-alone Titles
Ambition and Passion
Maison Angelique

Harrow Series
Wild Spirit
Wild Destiny
Wild Tempest
Wild Fire

Sandy Bay Series
Secrets in Sandy Bay
Escape to Sandy Bay
Return to Sandy Bay

GLOSSARY

Note that Australian English is used in this book. Spellings will be different to standard spelling used in the United States. Some of the terminology may be unfamiliar to readers outside of Australia.

Billy	Short for billycan, a metal pot used to boil water over an open fire
Bloke	Guy, man
Brolly	Umbrella
Coldie	Cold drink, usually beer.
Dead horse	Rhyming slang for Tomato Sauce
Mozzies	Mosquitoes
Piccaninny	Aboriginal baby
Piccaninny Dawn	First light, just before dawn
Shopping Trolley	Shopping Cart
Station	Ranch, large farming property in rural Australia
Uluru	Ayers Rock
Ute, Utility	Pickup

Thank you to Jessica for her enthusiastic support throughout my writing journey.

CHAPTER 1

THE NEEDLE HOVERED over empty on the gauge. Kathy's eyes alternated between the instrument and the darkening horizon. She was positive she had started the flight with adequate fuel. How far to her destination? She tried to do the calculations but her brain had frozen. Nothing made sense. She eased back on the throttle to eke more distance from the tank.

The man beside her shifted in his seat. She hadn't told him anything but the instrument panel was in front of him. If he looked at the fuel gauge, he could see for himself.

With great effort, she kept a blank face, hoping to hide her inner turmoil. She tried to act calm, not wanting to alarm him. The thump of her heart reflected her panic. Was it as loud as it felt? Could he hear it? Her hands were cold and clammy on the controls, in contrast to her face which was flushed. Beads of perspiration prickled her brow. The rumbling sensation in the pit of her stomach was ominous.

A belligerent voice interrupted her thoughts.

"How long have you held your licence? Not very long it seems."

She flicked him a glance, not wanting to break contact with the control panel. When she'd picked up the passenger, he'd looked interesting in a rugged sort of way. His physique indicated an active lifestyle, and he had an air of confident assurance. The grey eyes had barely looked in her direction then, but now they bored into her with intensity.

"Long enough." She didn't have to justify herself to him or to anyone else.

"You must have missed the class on fuel management. You realise we're approaching last light? There's nowhere around here to land in the dark—that much I do know."

"I don't understand. We had full fuel on take-off. I know we did." She tried to keep the panic out of her voice.

"Did you do a visual check? Bloody hell, I'm at the mercy of a total novice!" His grim face reflected the tone of his words. She didn't respond. Nothing she could say would change their situation. Could the gauge be wrong? Could they still have plenty of fuel and instead have an electrical problem? The fact that other gauges registered correctly didn't support this theory. Her heart sank with the needle.

The horizon grew fainter with the dwindling day. The procedurally correct action was to make a forced landing while she still had power and visibility. She could taste the bile rising at the thought of it.

The engine coughed. Hastily, she pushed in the mixture lever, hoping to keep it turning over.

"We'll never make the airport. Aim for the road, woman, aim for the road!"

His harsh voice cut across her concentration. As she peered below, trying to locate the road, the engine cut out completely, the propeller windmilling in ever slowing arcs.

"You won't get us out of this. I'm taking over!"

He seized the dual controls in front of him and the nose bucked in response.

"No!" she screamed. "Leave it alone."

He pulled, while she pushed. He was stronger; the nose edged dangerously higher. The fuselage shuddered as air speed washed away. The stall warning screamed and the aircraft pitched forward and started to spin. She kicked frantically at the rudder, trying to regain control. He jammed his feet on the pedals, locking them rigid. The ground rushed towards them. Her breath came in short, sharp bursts. This was how it would to end. Her life had only just begun. The unfairness and horror overwhelmed her. With mouth open in silent scream, she shut her eyes in the face of the inevitable.

Kathy gasped as her eyes jerked open. She could still feel the rocking movement. Her heart raced, and in her confusion, it took a while to work out where she was. She had splashed out on a sleeping compartment, but it had been a far from restful night. She woke periodically and had been aware of the noises and movement of the train. The built-up anticipation hadn't helped.

The dream left her feeling drained. She didn't need a dream therapist to tell her it was a reflection of her fears and anxieties. She pushed them aside. It was only a dream—

remember that. *Only a dream.* As her mother used to say, dreams were a way of processing your fears.

Nearly in Alice Springs—how surreal. Most of her anxieties related to the new job.

Pete was the one who'd thought she might not be up to the role. He'd been her flying instructor, and they'd developed a close relationship. Kathy would miss him, but not his claustrophobic attention, and she had jumped at this opportunity. She knew Pete's opposition had a personal basis and he'd maintained a vocal campaign.

"Kathy, you can't possibly understand the stresses and hardships you might come up against. It's not like city flying!"

"I hope it isn't. I've spent all this time, not to mention a small fortune in training and if that's where I'm offered a job then that's where I'll go. What was it Amelia Earhart said— *When a great adventure's offered, you don't refuse it.*"

Pete had snorted. "Well, it's not exactly launching off across the Pacific, but that remote country can be just as unforgiving if anything goes wrong."

She'd not listened to his opinions, or anyone else's for that matter. By the time the first sitting was called for breakfast, she was recovered, dressed and ready to go. She spent the rest of the journey watching the passing landscape, and wondering what awaited her when the train rolled into Alice that afternoon.

She soon found out. The contrast from the air-conditioned train was dramatic. The back of her throat gagged on the warm intensity. The choking air was dust-laden. She could smell it, taste it even. Kathy flicked a strand of hair off her face, already beaded with perspiration. Somebody must have slipped bricks into her bags when she wasn't looking. Dumping the luggage on the ground, she eased the ache in her fingers. For the first time, a creeping doubt surfaced. She'd refused to acknowledge any before, even to herself. Whatever she'd imagined, it hadn't been this stifling chaos.

"Watch out!"

She swung around and saw she had stopped in the path of a man walking behind her. He'd stumbled against her bags.

"Sorry."

She stooped to pick them up again, aware of a cool and dispassionate review. He didn't look enthralled. Tall, and wearing the moleskins, boots and hat that branded him a local, the man pushed past her with a murmured comment she couldn't quite decipher. Probably just as well.

"You should've looked where you were going," Kathy muttered.

"Sorry," she called again in the direction of his back. He half looked around with a brief nod and continued pushing through the throng of people. She saw him greet an attractive woman with a perfunctory kiss, and pick up her luggage before they disappeared into the mob. They looked a well-matched couple. *Wish someone would pick up my bags.*

The air conditioning of the station might have offered respite from the heat, but the crush of people rendered it virtually ineffective. As agreed, she looked near the ticketing counter for the woman who was meeting her. She scanned faces. No one in the crowd paid her any attention. She dragged her hair out of her eyes in irritation. *Just as well I didn't ask her to carry a newspaper. The town probably doesn't even have one!*

Setting down the luggage—carefully this time—she glanced around and massaged the ache in her fingers.

"Kathy?"

Turning, she saw a mass of bubbling copper curls above a freckled nose and a wide grin. *Could this possibly be the office manager?*

"Good trip? The train's quite an experience, isn't it? It's not far to the car. Here, give me one of your bags."

Kathy followed as the woman grasped a bag and pushed her way through the crowd. If she didn't keep up, both her bag and this woman might be swallowed by the swirling mass of people. The grin turned momentarily back in her direction.

"I'm Sarah, by the way. Welcome to Alice!"

With the bags stashed in the back of Gordon, which was the name of Sarah's obviously well-loved but slightly battered station wagon, Kathy took stock of the young woman before her. She was short and comfortably rounded, and somehow it looked right on her. The smattering of freckles which dusted the pert nose gave her grin an air of cheekiness.

She was momentarily distracted from this evaluation when she noticed that the man from the platform had parked adjacent to them. She felt those eyes on her again. The slight pause as he loaded his car indicated he had recognised her. Now she could see him clearly, she felt a vague sense of recognition. Perhaps he looked like someone else she knew. It might come to her later. She gave an apologetic smile, but there was no response. *Too bad, his loss.* She turned her attention back to Sarah.

"We're driving to the top of Anzac Hill first," said Sarah as they climbed into the car. "I thought you might like to get your bearings. It's rather special at this time of day."

Kathy was mystified, but not for long. Anzac Hill lay at the northern end of the town, and was accessible via a steep winding road, with a set of concrete stairs completing the final ascent. At the apex, an obelisk pierced the skies as a memorial to the young men who'd fought for their country on foreign shores.

A spectacular view awaited them, with the town laid out in neat orderly rows below. The suburbs were not so disciplined. Their shape and form were modified by the tree-studded river course, and other hills, similar to this one but smaller. The peaks challenged the landscape presenting a strong environment.

Dusk in the outback was hard to describe. As the heat of the day dissipated, the birds began their evening calls, and the colours of the sky softly changed. Kathy saw subtle hues of pinks, oranges and violet spread across the horizon, bathing both the clouds and the backdrop of the MacDonnell Ranges with a delicate light that was magical. As the crickets joined in with their evening song, speech seemed superfluous. She caught her breath.

"This is stunning! I never imagined Alice Springs would look like this."

"It doesn't all the time. In the heat of midday, with a dust storm blanketing the town, it's hard to remember just how beautiful it can be. It's not called the Red Heart for nothing."

Sarah made a sweeping gesture at the scene below, turning to look at Kathy.

"All I need do is to come up here at sunset, and experience these moments again. It reaffirms my sense of identity with the place."

An evening breeze stirred the two women as they paused to admire the view over the Telegraph Station Reserve that had been behind them, before making their way back to the car.

Driving back down the road that gave access to the summit of the hill, another car passed them on the way up. Kathy couldn't be sure from the passing glimpse, but it looked like the man from the railway station. Odd, she thought, to see him yet again. If she were the suspicious type, she would think he was following her. That was silly, because they'd not seen each other before that afternoon.

Sarah pulled up outside a large, low-slung bungalow, explaining it had been subdivided into four flats. The wide veranda across the front and along both sides gave protection to all entrances, and the outdoor furniture positioned on one side veranda indicated an extension of the indoor living areas.

"Everyone who lives here works for StationAir. The veranda's a favourite spot for a get-together after work—a drink and a chat. It's not bad for breakfast on a Sunday morning either. That's usually a combined effort. Someone provides a pot of coffee, and someone else the fruit or croissants or whatever."

Sarah led the way to a doorway on the side of the house, and setting down the suitcase she'd carried in from the car, searched through her pockets until she found the key.

"Well, this is it; Chez Kathy!"

She opened the door with a flourish and stood back for Kathy to enter.

"I've stocked your fridge with a few basics to tide you over until you can do your own shopping. Dinner tonight is on me. My flat is at the front of the house, so it's not far to come."

"Thanks, Sarah."

Kathy looked around, taking stock of the place that was to be her new home.

"I didn't expect to be looked after like this. Are you sure dinner won't be too much trouble?"

"Of course not! If I'm throwing one steak on the grill, it's not much trouble to throw on another."

The grin was now more of a conspiratorial smile. "It will be nice to have some female company. The guys are great to work with, but female back-up and support will be much appreciated!"

Moving towards the door, she added, "You'd probably like to have a shower, and do some unpacking. Come around to my flat at about six, and by then I'll have dinner well on the way."

❧

"Door's open—come in!" Sarah's voice emerged from behind the screen door.

Kathy opened the door, welcomed by a tantilising smell. She'd showered once Sarah had left, revelling in the jets of water that washed away the heat and dust. The showers on the train were small and cramped, and feeling guilty about others awaiting their turn, she hadn't liked to linger. Now that she'd freshened up and got a few things sorted, she was more interested in food.

The kitchen appeared to be in a state of organised chaos. The makings of a salad were already in a bowl, and Sarah was whisking a dressing. Bottles of oil and condiments sat on the kitchen bench, and Kathy was impressed that Sarah was a d-iy kind of woman. Peering at the salad, she could see it contained slices of peach and pistachio nuts. Yum.

"Can I help?" queried Kathy as Sarah made for the stove, turning the sizzling steaks.

"You could open the bottle of wine. We should celebrate your first night in the Alice. It's in the fridge, and you'll find glasses in the cupboard to your right."

Kathy poured them each a glass of wine while Sarah flipped the steaks onto plates, and they took their places at the table. The aroma of the steak was tantalizing. Kathy tentatively tried a mouthful.

"Oh, this is good! I didn't expect it to be so tender."

"One of the perks of this job is access to station beef. It has a unique flavour. Tonight's meal is compliments of Mulga Downs."

"What and where is Mulga Downs?" she asked, pausing to sip some wine.

"It's one of the stations on the North-East mail run. The route will be one of your responsibilities. The property is managed by Alex Woodleigh, the third generation of his family to do so. We take out mail and any supplies or equipment they've ordered, and on occasion, the odd passenger. You're always sure of a cup of tea at Mulga, and as you can see, sometimes the odd meat parcel as well."

"I thought you worked in the office?"

"I do, but if it's quiet, and if I think the receptionist can cope with any minor crises, I sometimes sneak along for the ride. It depends how much extra luggage is being carried, or whether or not any passengers are on board. We carry station people who and sometimes tourists book on the runs as well. I haven't struck one yet who didn't thoroughly enjoy it."

"I suppose you get quite a few tourists through the region?"

"We do. Uluru has always been a draw card, and then of course that sad incident a couple of years ago with the dingo and Azaria Chamberlain brought additional notoriety to the area. It's a bucket-list destination for many people."

It had been on Kathy's bucket list too. Hopefully she wouldn't have to carry any tourists until she was familiar with the route and knew what she was supposed to be doing. Her parents might enjoy the flight when they came up on their promised visit. Her father would appreciate the opportunity to try station beef.

"Well, the steak's good, but you're a great cook. I'll have to brush up on my culinary skills if I'm to survive around here. My repertoire is basic at best."

"I wouldn't worry. As the new girl in town, you'll get lots of attention. There are heaps of restaurants in Alice, and before long you'll have tried every one of them!"

Kathy shook her head. "I'm more concerned with settling in and finding my feet than in socialising," she replied. "Anyway, this is a contract role. I may not be here very long."

She was rewarded with that grin again.

"Perhaps, but you might as well make the most of it while you're here. There's a great social life, and with the absence of the city cultural activities, we make our own entertainment. Soon it will seem as though you've been in Alice forever.

Sarah cleared their plates from the table and set about making a pot of coffee and placing cups and a jug of milk on a tray. The plate with Tim Tams indicated the basis for some of her curves.

"Come on. We'll have our coffee on the veranda. It will be pleasant out there. If you can open the door, I'll carry the tray out."

The temperature had dropped to a soft balmy level, and a gentle breeze carried with it the scent of the frangipani tree in the front yard. The angst Kathy had felt on arrival had settled. She still found it hard to believe she was in the middle of Australia. It wasn't what she had expected. What other surprises lay in store?

The two women settled back comfortably. The chairs had seen better days, and probably took a battering from the extremes of weather, but they served their purpose.

"I'm surprised we haven't had company by now," observed Sarah. "There are two guys in each of the other two flats, and I didn't think they would contain their curiosity about you this long. It's not every day a female pilot joins the firm."

"Surely they won't make a big deal about the gender issue?"

"They may watch you closely for a while, but they'll settle down."

Kathy wasn't sure whether to feel relieved or disconcerted.

"What about the passengers?" she queried. "Will I get any adverse reaction from them?"

"Nah. They've got two choices: they can fly with you, or they can walk. Up to them."

Kathy didn't even try to suppress her grin. She would enjoy working with Sarah.

"And people from the stations?"

"Generally, they'll give anyone a fair go. If they see you're competent, then they'll treat you accordingly. They're down to earth."

Sarah sipped her coffee.

The crickets had worked themselves up to full evensong, and a bevy of moths battered themselves with monotonous regularity against the veranda light.

"You'll soon meet the locals. I imagine you'll have to do just as much adjusting as they will. They all have a story to tell. Take Mum Gardner for instance. She runs Bindaroo Station. She has done since her husband died some twenty years ago, leaving her with two little kids. Mum's as tough as nails, and has never had a day's rest since, but she has a heart of gold."

Before continuing, she offered the plate of Tim Tams to Kathy, who only hesitated a moment before taking one.

"If anyone's in trouble, she's the first to provide a helping hand and there always seems to be extra mouths at her kitchen table. The boys are old enough to run things themselves now but Mum still rules the roost. They can be fair devils at times, but Mum soon pulls them into line!"

"She sounds intriguing. From what you've described, if I put the slightest foot wrong, she might tear strips off me!"

"Not Mum. If anyone is likely to tear strips off you, it will be Alex Woodleigh."

"Really? Why would he do that?"

"Alex is the tall, dark, handsome and arrogant type. He has a blunt style of communication, but gets away with it. He's fairly well respected in these parts."

Sarah pursed her lips thoughtfully, head tilted to one side in reflection.

"He doesn't suffer fools gladly. When he turns that penetrating gaze on me, I feel as though I'm all thumbs. If I can drop something or trip over it, I will!"

She gave a heartfelt sigh. "The worst part is, he's the best-looking man for miles around and up here, that's really saying something. He's single too, and definitely eligible. You remember I told you over dinner that he's the owner of Mulga Downs, but he rarely gives the women from town a second glance. He's polite and courteous, but I have the feeling they don't quite measure up. To what, I don't know."

"Perhaps he's not interested in women. Has that occurred to you?"

Sarah gave a hoot of laughter. "He's certainly not that way inclined. He does pay some attention to Melissa Gilbert, and she definitely pays a lot of attention to him!"

"Isn't she a local then?"

"Yes, and no. Melissa lives on Plenty River Station, which is a neighbouring property to Mulga Downs. She went to boarding school, but otherwise she's lived most of her life on the station. She's one of these women who lives in the saddle and is perfectly at home in the stock camp, but looks just as good in a slinky evening dress at the Cattlemen's Ball."

"She sounds very adaptable."

"In that sense, yes. She's not terribly friendly in town though, so in some ways, she and Alex are two of a kind. She seems to have some antiquated idea of landed gentry and all that, as though she is a cut above the rest of us. Anyway, she and Alex come from a similar background, and understand each other's lifestyle so I guess they're well suited."

Sarah viewed her guest with open curiosity.

"And what about you? Did you leave any broken hearts behind in Adelaide?"

"Not at all. I've invested too much in my career to get diverted by relationships. I've come to Alice looking to broaden my experience, but of the professional kind only. Happy to socialize, and from what you've described there's plenty of opportunity, but I'm not looking for any complications. Keep it simple, that's my motto."

"Mm," Sarah replied reflectively. "There's something to be said for that."

They drifted into a contemplative silence. The headlights of a car swung into the driveway, and were then extinguished. A door slammed, and Kathy heard a steady pair of footsteps coming in their direction.

Sarah turned, shielding her eyes from the veranda light as she peered into the darkness.

"Brian! Come and meet your new colleague. Kathy, this is Brian, one of your co-pilots. In fact, I think you'll be going out with him tomorrow."

The man stepped into the circle of light. He wore a check shirt over a pair of jeans, with comfortable rather than startling looks. He extended a hand with a welcoming smile, and grasped Kathy's in a firm shake.

"Pleased to meet you, Kathy. Sorry I wasn't around earlier, but I'm sure Sarah has taken good care of you."

"She's done more than that. She's wined and dined me, and now she's filling me in on some of the people I'm likely to meet."

"Well, whatever she has told you about me, it's all true, only I'm twice as good."

"The conceit of the man! As a matter of fact, I hadn't told Kathy anything about you yet."

"I see. Leaving the best until last, were you?"

Sarah turned to Kathy with a mock despairing shrug. "You can see what I have to put up with, working with these blokes. Now you can understand why I'm delighted to have another woman around."

"I don't think it's such a bad idea myself." Brian said, his admiring glance bold in its appraisal.

Kathy was glad that the poor light hid the sudden flush she could feel on her cheeks. She smiled sweetly. "Female pilots do have superior aviating skills. I guess that's why I got the job."

"Hm! There might be interesting times ahead." he said.

She smiled. "I'm sure we'll make a great team, and I'll be grateful for any help you can give me. You are right about one thing. The next few days are going to be an interesting experience, and I have a feeling it's going to be mostly for me!"

With this last thought in mind, Kathy decided to turn in. It had been a long day, and she was anxious to be fully rested by morning. Exchanging final pleasantries, and making arrangements with Brian for a lift in the morning, she bade them both good night and returned to her flat.

Sliding into bed and under the light covers, she reviewed the last few hours. Sarah had been helpful, and had done a lot to put her at ease, but this was her first real flying job. She wouldn't admit the small dose of nerves undermining her confidence to anyone. She drifted into sleep, with dreams interspersed with rumbling trains, planes, and vast open spaces.

CHAPTER 2

NO ALARM REQUIRED. Kathy woke at the crack of dawn, feeling far from rested. Her brain flitted in all directions, thinking about the new job and what might lie before her. She wished she could switch it off.

Sighing, she levered herself out of bed. A shower perked her up but she knew nervous energy would carry her through the day.

What to wear was not a problem as she already had the corporate uniform. Her flying clothes consisted of light blue shirts, both short and long-sleeved, navy-blue slacks or a navy-blue skirt, with a navy jumper for cooler weather. Shoes were sensible leather slip-ons, in regulation black.

She surveyed herself in the mirror. She wanted to look her best for her first day, without resorting to make-up. She settled for a generous application of her moisturiser containing sun block, lip gloss and a light coating of mascara, the latter lengthening and darkening her long eyelashes. For good luck as much as anything, she also added a dab of light perfume behind her ears and to the pulse spots.

With swift steady strokes, she brushed her golden hair, so fine that it sparkled and crackled with static electricity. She gathered it in a sleek pony tail and secured it with a blue ribbon. This strategy, she hoped, would give a groomed finish in spite of those little wispy bits that always shook themselves free to float at will.

She looked professional and business-like. After a hasty breakfast of fruit and yoghurt, she gave herself one last inspection, and hurried around to Brian's flat.

Brian gave her a brief run-down in the company van on StationAir; the people who were employed, the type of aircraft they flew and detail on the routes she could expect to be flying. The commentary expanded on the conversation that she'd had with Sarah the night before.

StationAir had an office in the town, as well as flight offices, a reception area and hangars out at the airport. Most of the administrative staff were employed in the town office. This was the centre for collecting freight and handling passenger enquiries, as well as attending to other administrative affairs. The day was already heating up and small beads of perspiration broke out on her face. The office was a welcome contrast.

Brian led Kathy past the reception area to a suite of offices beyond. Pausing at an open door, he knocked before entering. The man studying the charts on the wall looked around. He was thickset, with a ruddy complexion that told of years in the sun. He looked inquiringly at Brian, until he saw the figure hesitating behind.

"Kathy!" he exclaimed. "Come in. Brian, there's a delivery just come in for Bundy. Perhaps you could check the manifest. You'll be doing the trip out there this afternoon. On the way back, you need to swing past Mulga Downs and pick up one of the station hands who needs to come into town for dental treatment. There's one thing you can say about Alex Woodleigh—he knows how to look after his employees."

Where have I heard that name? Oh yes—he was the one who Sarah described last night. He sounds like someone to treat with caution.

"Okay Boss."

Brian left the room and Kathy turned to face her new employer. She had met Rob Collins in Adelaide, at the initial job interview. He gestured to a chair.

"Welcome aboard. This morning, you can come out to the airport with me and I'll check you out on the two-ten. That's the aircraft that you'll usually be flying, but in time you'll do an endorsement on the Paternavia."

The two-ten he referred to was a Cessna high wing six-seater aircraft, designated because of engine capacity as a C210. Kathy already knew they were good work-horse aircraft for use in the outback. They carried a reasonable amount of luggage and were suitable for operating out of the bush strips. She had expected to be checked out on arrival and at regular periods there-after.

"This afternoon, you can go with Brian on the run to Bundy. Until you find your feet in this country, I'll send you out in tandem with other pilots. That way you can familiarise yourself with the scenery, and the boys will introduce you at the route destinations and show you the ropes."

His tone changed to one that was all business. He turned back to the charts on the wall, lines indicating the routes normally flown. He stabbed a finger in their direction.

"While you're doing these flights, I want you to take pencil and paper, and draw a mud-map of every airstrip you see, and position it in relation to the neighbouring hills, river, stock pens, homestead—anything at all that might help physically identify that particular strip. It's an old practice out this way. It's one way of effectively committing a location and its layout to memory, which is useful if visibility becomes impaired due to weather, or you become—" there was a telling pause "temporarily unsure of your location."

Kathy was familiar with the euphemism for 'lost', and hoped she never found herself in that situation.

With the serious part of the discussion over, Rob took her on a guided tour of the office, introducing her to staff encountered along the way. A few curious glances were cast in her direction, and she was glad when she found Sarah's welcoming grin firmly established for the day in the main office.

"If you've finished with Kathy for now Boss, I'll fill her in on the important things, like where the coffee's kept, and where she can sit when she's in town."

Rob Collins nodded. "She's all yours. I'll leave her in your capable hands. Give Kathy a copy of the two-ten handling notes and also the local charts she is likely to need. If you'd like to go over those, Kathy, we'll leave for the airport in about half an hour."

With a cup of coffee in one hand, and a bundle of maps, charts and notes in the other, Kathy settled herself at the desk she had been allocated, and tried to cram in as much in the next half hour as she could. She asked Sarah to pin-point Bundy for her, and studied the route carefully. She had a lot to learn and this was the time to start.

With the 'clear to take-off' command issued by the tower, Kathy eased the plane onto the run-way. She lined up with the centre line and firmly pushed the throttle forward. Being a hot day, she didn't experience a coltish leap into the air. Rather there was the gradual awareness that the ground was being left behind. The rate of climb was slow given the high temperature, and she kept the nose pushed low to build up airspeed before settling into the climb.

Rob directed her out to the training area. There, he put her through her paces. She did steep turns, put the aircraft into a stall, went through a forced landing procedure, and did some simulated instrument flying.

To her relief, all manoeuvres were completed with text-book precision. Each aircraft has its own idiosyncrasies, and to coax an unfamiliar plane through its paces can be a challenging experience. She breathed a sigh of relief as they headed back to the airport, and joined the circuit pattern.

Rob had not finished with her. Some bush strips were less than perfect, he explained, so he made her do a short-field landing and then a short field take-off, followed finally by a landing without the aircraft flaps being lowered. All his requests were accomplished competently and accurately.

Pulling up outside the StationAir hanger, Rob took her inside to introduce her to the mechanics. Various aircraft with their engine covers off and innards exposed, were being worked on by a group of men clad in brightly-coloured overalls. A radio blared in one corner, and two of the men, cheerfully if somewhat tunelessly, sang along with the latest release. They seemed a happy crew.

Kathy paused at the entrance, waiting for her eyes to adjust after being in the bright sunlight. Slowly, the interior of the hangar came into focus. Direct and appraising stares greeted her. Feeling a slow flush spread across her face, she wasn't sure whether to smile in response or feign casual indifference.

As she was deliberating the question, Rob Collins called out, "All right you lot, behave! This is Kathy Sullivan, and I don't want you scaring her off on her first day with us."

"Aw Boss, you know us! We wouldn't scare a pussy cat!"

The speaker had a flaming carrot thatch above blue-green eyes. With freckles liberally applied all over his face, and dressed in a pair of sky-blue overalls, he resembled a mischievous pixie as he stood hands on hips, head on one side, surveying the visitors.

"So, you're the new receptionist, are you, love?"

Kathy looked at him sharply. She thought from what Sarah had said, people knew she was starting as one of the air crew.

There was a silence. Eyes swivelled in her direction. Coolly assessing those that gleamed in front of her, Kathy realised the man was stirring. He knew quite well who and what she was.

"Actually," she smiled sweetly, "I'm the new Safety Inspector from the Department of Aviation. I'm here to do a safety audit, and to check on your procedures."

A fleeting look of surprise crossed his face before he threw back his head and roared with laughter.

"A wise guy, no less! No worries, I think you will find us all in order."

She shook hands firmly with Colin and the rest of the crew, aware that her check flight that morning had not been the only test she passed. As they moved to office at the side of the hanger, Rob Collins spoke as an aside.

"Don't let them fluster you, Kathy. They're not above having a stir, as you've seen for yourself, but give as good as you get, and you'll get along fine. They're also very competent, and together they're a good team."

"If that's the worst teasing I get, I'll have an easy time of it."

They found Brian in the office, checking some paper work. He looked up, acknowledging their return.

"Brian," directed Rob. "I'm sending Kathy out to Bundy with you this afternoon. Show her the manifests and the loading procedures, and point out anything else she needs to know along the way."

"No worries. I'm about to grab some lunch from the airport cafeteria. Kathy, if you want to come too, I'll show you our route when we get back here, and you can do the flight plan."

Kathy realised she was hungry. Wonderful how calming flying could be for the nerves! "That's fine by me," she answered with a quick smile. "Lead on."

Their aircraft, one of the company's C210s, had been refuelled while they were having lunch. All that remained was for the loading to be completed, and for the flight plan to be filled out and filed with the Briefing Office. While Brian attended to the loading, Kathy tackled the flight plan, glad she had taken the opportunity to study the route. Verifying some of the information with Brian, she filled in the appropriate details as required for their journey and then slipped down to the airport Briefing Office to get the latest weather information.

The walls of the office were covered in various charts, maps and diagrams. A large L-shaped counter separated the public from the 'working' side of the room. There was only one other person there filing a plan. Judging by his clothing, he was from out of town. His jeans ended in R.M. Williams boots, and the open necked casual shirt was kept firmly tucked in by a hand-tooled leather belt.

One end of the counter was the domain of the meteorologists. She approached the Met Man with a bright smile.

"Afternoon! I'd like an area forecast please."

"Certainly—for which area?"

Australia was divided into different numbered forecast areas, with a different report prepared for each individual area. She could have kicked herself.

"Ah... sorry, I didn't check exactly which one I needed. This is my first day here, and I usually—"

"Why am I not surprised? You usually have someone else to hold your hand."

Kathy spun around to find she was being addressed by the man she'd noticed as when she entered. He was taller than she'd first thought, and her eyes widened as he moved closer, forcing her to look up at him. At that proximity, she could smell a combination of soap, leather and something else indefinable. There was no friendliness in the eyes regarding her. She recognised the man from the railway station. What a weird coincidence, running into him again.

"I beg your pardon?" She used her best 'don't mess with me voice'.

"You city pilots are all the same! You blunder up here without doing your homework, come inadequately prepared, and then expect the locals to spend time and money looking for you when you get yourselves lost. I'd take yourself back home. This isn't the sort of country to get lost in. You can't even navigate your way through a railway station."

She was floored by the unexpected diatribe, but quickly gathered her wits.

"As it happens," she enunciated slowly and icily, "I'm qualified to fly here or anywhere else. Flying happens to be my job. Neither you, nor anyone else, will have to come looking for me."

She stood her ground, her heart pounding but determined all the same not to be intimidated. He was nasty; no other word for it. "Perhaps *you* should have been looking where you were going. You should have apologised for running into me."

She held his gaze for two beats, then deliberately turned her back on him, and started looking through her charts. She could sense him still looking at her. Her breath quickened in annoyance. What was he doing?

"Don't tell me this is who's replacing Dave Bishop? Lord help us. What an insult."

The words were spoken softly and Kathy wasn't quite sure she had heard correctly. What did he mean and who was she replacing?

"Couldn't find a husband in the city I suppose," mused the man, a little louder. She was clearly meant to hear. "Can't think what else would bring an inexperienced young woman to the outback to work."

Keep calm, Kathy said to herself. *The man is a moron and not worth getting upset over.*

She found the information she needed and asked the Met Man for an Area 85 report and an aerodrome forecast. Taking the printed sheets, she turned and smiled artfully.

"Of course; how transparent of me! I didn't think my plans were quite so obvious. But then, when the Centre is populated by charming and friendly men such as you, I am amazed the town isn't besieged by hordes of single women in search of a husband. Now, if you will excuse me—my ulterior motives will have to be put on hold. I've a flight to plan!"

She moved to the desk that was set aside for pilot use, and studied the forecasts she had been given. Or rather, tried to. The coded text morphed into mumbo jumbo in front of her eyes, and to her annoyance, she knew her face had flushed bright red. She was aware of the man standing behind her, although she was determined not to give him further acknowledgement.

"Well even in the marriage stakes," he drawled "I doubt you'll have much luck. Living in this sort of country takes commitment, and flying out here's not a picnic. You won't stick it out long enough to get a ring on your finger."

Kathy flushed in outrage. Just *what* was his problem? Not that she was going to ask him. She didn't get the chance, because he didn't wait for a response.

Striding to the door, he turned back to face the men behind the counter.

"Phil—I forgot to congratulate you on the new baby. Well done to you and the missus, mate."

He spun on his heel and strode out, leaving a stunned silence behind him.

As Kathy looked around, several pairs of eyes hastily averted themselves, and everyone suddenly seemed very busy. She knew they had heard every word. She completed the final details on her flight plan and resolutely fronted up to the counter. She looked the briefing officer full in the eye, as though daring him to make a comment.

He cleared his throat uncomfortably. "Hi. I gather you're the latest recruit to StationAir." He gave an apologetic shrug. "Welcome to Alice."

Kathy let out a pent-up breath. She handed over her flight plan with a smile that belied her inner distress.

"Perhaps, given that I am new to Alice and unfamiliar with local procedures, you might like to take particular care in checking my entries." Her bantering tone brought a corresponding smile.

"It looks fine to me. After all, the regulations are the same, no matter where you are. Stick by them and you won't have any problems."

He recorded some key information and handed back the form with a smile.

"If you have any queries, don't hesitate to ask. I think you'll find *most* people only too willing to help. Have a good flight."

Feeling re-assured by this exchange, Kathy pushed the earlier unpleasantness from her mind, and hurried back towards the hangar area. It occurred to her that given she had encountered her antagonist in the briefing office, he must have been lodging a flight plan as well. If that was the case, he was probably somewhere nearby.

As she scanned the light aircraft parking area, an aircraft started up and taxied towards the runway. She could see who was at the controls. At least she wasn't going to run into him again while preparing for take-off.

Brian had finished loading the aircraft, and was doing a final check of fuel and oil levels.

"All set?"

She nodded, aware of the feeling of anticipation. This was what she'd been waiting for.

"We'd best be on our way then." He quickly polished the windscreen, and they climbed aboard. With a minimum of time and fuss, they were airborne and climbing out on track for Bundy.

Having flown the route many times before, Brian methodically completed preliminary flight checks, and then settled back in his seat. He was able to point out homesteads and geographical features along the way that he thought might be of interest. There were so many special stories attached to the places and the people who lived in them. Kathy was enchanted, both by the travelogue, and by the country that moved steadily under them.

Swiftly sketching local airstrips and features of interest as Rob Collins had earlier instructed, she couldn't help but marvel at the beauty of this antique land. The landscape didn't present the pristine sort of beauty that one would find on a chocolate box, and it wouldn't appeal to everyone, but there was something arresting about the country just the same. She said as much to Brian, and was a little surprised when he dropped the now familiar light-hearted tone.

"I could never tire of this place; I just love it.

He glanced away from the view beyond the cowling and looked at Kathy with a rueful smile.

"I wasn't too keen on coming here when I first got the job. I thought I'd probably only stay for a while before moving on. I still want to further my flying career of course, so eventually I'll have to leave, but the place sort of grew on me. When I have to go, it will be a wrench."

Kathy nodded acknowledgement. "I've only just arrived, but I think I understand what you mean. I'm going to enjoy getting to know the Centre. There's an attraction even I can feel after such a short time."

"A tail wind has given us time up our sleeve. I can show you a few of the local scenic attractions."

Disengaging the autopilot, he deviated from track and reduced height before taking them skimming low over the Elkedra River. Kathy had thought that all the rivers in the Centre were just dry sandy beds, so she was delighted to find that this one held water. Apparently, some of the water holes were permanent too, and with recent rains, the river had been flowing again. The water holes had been flushed out, and fresh green growth was visible along the banks. The greatest surprise of all was the number of birds that were swimming and nesting along the river and among the reeds. Brian didn't know what sort they were, possibly ibises he told her, whilst Kathy even spotted a Pelican.

"Okay," said Brian said after a moment. "We're not far from Bundy now so we'd better get back on track. Tighten your seat belt and raise your tray table. Cabin crew, prepare for landing!"

As Brian commenced the let down towards the homestead, Kathy could see a low cluster of buildings, some of them surrounded by lawn. Brian explained there were several houses besides the main homestead, and these were where the station hands and their families lived. Other buildings were the school room, the store, and general outhouses.

On top of a nearby hill, Kathy could see a white saucer-shaped dish mounted on a stand and asked Brian about it.

"It's the station's satellite dish. That gives them access to television broadcasts and means they don't have to rely on radio telephone for their phone calls."

"Do all properties have them?" The mechanics of communication in the outback was something she hadn't considered.

"Not yet. They're expensive to install, but as there's greater take-up and they become cheaper, those barriers of isolation will be either reduced or even removed."

They circled the homestead before heading for the strip. The cloud of dust that followed them along the track from the group of buildings indicated they had been seen, and someone was driving out to the strip to meet them.

The landing was sure and smooth, and as the plane slowed out of its landing roll, it arrived at the end of the strip at the same time as the vehicle.

With the engine shut down, the pair climbed out and stretched. A tall, lanky man unwound himself from the utility.

"G'day Brian. Right on time I see. Got yerself a new off-sider?" He threw a quizzical glance at Kathy.

"Bob, I'd like you to meet Kathy Sullivan. This is Kathy's first day flying for StationAir. I'm showing her the ropes."

"Is that so? Well, yer different to the last bloke. I guess that won't be a problem. Pleased t' meet yer, miss."

Kathy stepped forward, and offered her hand. The look of consternation on Bob's face told her that he was not used to shaking hands with young women. Good manners, however rough, won the day. Carefully wiping his hand on the back of his jeans first, Bob obliged by taking her hand in his work-calloused palm. Kathy resisted the urge to give his hand a hearty squeeze in return.

She did baulk when he wanted to unload the aircraft instead of her. "It's *my* job," she insisted firmly, determined not to let either man think she was incapable of doing her share. She sorted the freight in the rear of the aircraft and selected the items that were labelled for Bundy.

"That was quick. Would yer like to come up t' the house for a cup of tea?" Bob's eyebrows were raised questioningly.

Brian threw a quick glance at Kathy before answering for both of them. "Thanks Bob, but we'd better keep going. We've still got a passenger to pick up from Mulga Downs. We should keep moving so that Kathy has time for a de-brief before clock off."

"Right-o then. We'll see you next time Kathy. See ya, Brian."

They swung the aircraft around on the strip, lined up and Brian gunned the engine for take-off, setting course this time for Mulga Downs.

On arrival at the station, Brian reduced height and flew a tight circle over the homestead before tracking towards the strip, some distance from the house. They saw a vehicle heading in their direction, and by the time they had joined the circuit area and landed, their passenger was waiting for them. Brian didn't even shut down.

Kathy climbed out and pushed her seat forward allowing their passenger to gain access to the back seat. With the man securely strapped in, she reclaimed her seat and closed and secured the door.

Introductions were shouted, and they all settled ready for take-off. The station vehicle returned along the route from which it had come, and the aircraft lifted into the air again and set course for Alice.

Engine noise made conversing with the passenger difficult, so after the initial exchanges, Kathy redirected her attention back to the front.

"Had enough for your first day?" Brian asked.

"I have. It's been a lot to take in but it's been good."

She reviewed the events of the day in her head. "Brian, who's Dave Bishop?"

There was a momentary silence. Brian cleared his throat, his gaze fixed on the horizon.

"Dave was a pilot with StationAir. Grew up in this area, so was well-known."

Kathy sensed there was more to the story. Glancing at Brian, she saw a hint of sadness in his expression. She waited, not wanting to push him.

"He developed leukemia. Not fair really, a good bloke like him. He put up a fight but it got him in the end. He died not long ago."

"Brian, I'm so sorry. I had no idea. It must have been devastating for you all."

"Those were sad days—especially for Sarah."

"Were they close?"

Another slight pause. "Yeah, you could say that. Indications were they were in it for the long haul. Sarah doesn't talk about it. She seems to have just clammed up, so we don't talk about it much either."

"Thanks for filling me in. I'll be careful what I say." *Poor Sarah. What an awful thing to happen.* Kathy couldn't imagine what she must have gone through.

"Is it true I've been employed in his place?"

"Well, it's a while now since Dave died," Brian said, "and we've all shouldered the load since then. The boss wasn't in a hurry to replace him and we were all grateful for that. Some time was needed to come to terms with how it affected people."

He chewed his lip, his expression indicating that he was one of those people.

"Work is building up and it has got to the point where another pilot is required, which is why this current contract has been offered to you. You're not a direct replacement but yes, you are filling a space that was left vacant by Dave."

"I see. I'm glad you've told me. It's helpful to know some of the background."

Life was sometimes more complex than you expected.

The rest of the flight back to Alice seemed to take no time at all. Their passenger left them with a wave and headed in the direction of a taxi from the airport car park. With the aircraft safely hangered, and paperwork left in the office, the pair climbed into Brian's van and headed into town.

"A few people are meeting up for a drink after work at the Hotel Alice. What say we drop in for a while? Sarah should be there too and some of the other StationAir people. Give you a chance to get to know them."

"Oh... sure, all right. We won't make a session of it though, will we?"

Kathy would have been just as happy to go straight home, climb under a nice hot shower, and relax, but appreciated that she needed to be sociable, especially on her first day.

She could hear Sarah before she saw her. The hotel had an inner courtyard and here, on outdoor furniture surrounded by planter boxes housing a variety of greenery, was gathered an assortment of people. Some of them Kathy recognised from passing introductions throughout the day. Even if she hadn't, she would have identified the right group by Sarah's strident laugh.

Conversation was cut short as the newcomers were spotted.

"Hi Kathy! Come and meet the crew. Everyone, this is Kathy. Who's going to buy her a drink? Can't have her thinking we're an unsociable lot. Come and sit here. Hey, Brian. Did you look after Kathy today?"

Everyone regarded her with curiosity. In the light of her new knowledge, she felt self-conscious. Were they comparing her, and weighing her up? There wasn't a lot that she could do if they were. Those she'd met earlier smiled and nodded, whilst the rest, taking a cue from Sarah, volunteered their names. They all seemed to be industry people, but not necessarily pilots, and not necessarily working with StationAir. Two of the men she was introduced to, Mark and Chris, were helicopter pilots, involved principally in aerial mustering. It sounded fascinating. Kathy had never flown in a helicopter. To learn to fly a rotary wing aircraft seemed the ultimate challenge.

"I heard someone say once that learning to fly a chopper is like learning to balance on top of a beach ball." she said.

Mark laughed. "That's a fair analogy I suppose, but we have been doing it for so long that it's become second nature. I don't even think about it anymore."

"You'll have to come for a flight with us," added Chris. "You could have a feel of the controls then, and judge for yourself."

"Could I? That would be fantastic." Kathy's eyes lit up. "On second thoughts, I'm not sure that I should. I might never be satisfied with flying fixed wing again."

Over the general laughter, Sarah demanded a run-down of her day. It had been full and eventful. Kathy told them about the mechanics out at the airport, and the people she met, and the water holes and the birds they saw on the way out to Bundy.

She didn't tell them about the incident in the Briefing Office. After all, she didn't know who the man was. His was probably best forgotten. Also, she didn't want to advertise that she had done something so basic as to forget to check on the required area classification.

Sipping her drink, and letting the surrounding noise and chatter wash over her, life in Adelaide seemed eons away. It surprised Kathy that her thoughts kept returning to the man from the briefing office. He was incredibly rude and had an attitude problem, so why couldn't she get him out of her mind?

CHAPTER 3

MUM GARDNER WAS as friendly as Sarah said she would be. She had driven out to the strip to meet them with a cheery "G'day love!"

Though her figure was matronly, she swung herself out of the Land Rover and strode over to meet them with a step as sprightly as a young girl's. She was clad in jeans and boots, and the battered leather hat she wore looked like an old and well-loved friend.

As Kathy had been told, Mum was still feminine for all the traditionally masculine work that she did. One of her habits was to always wear gloves when working to protect her hands and nails. She was not, and never intended to be 'one of the boys', and woe betide anyone who thought her working appearance was an automatic licensing of coarse liberties.

"You must be Kathy. Heard you were coming. I've been looking forward to meeting you." She beamed. "So good to see another woman out here. You'll have a cuppa before moving on, won't you?"

"Do we have time?" Kathy looked hesitantly towards Brian.

"You bet. I always have time for a cuppa with Mum. I don't suppose you've got any cake too?"

"I don't know… you boys must have hollow boots. Of course, I have cake. Make yourself useful and get the things out of the car while Kathy and I have a chat."

Kathy was bemused to see that Brian jumped to and did as he was told. This was obviously a regular event.

A folding picnic table with canvas chairs was removed from the vehicle, and set up in the shade of a Desert Oak. A wicker hamper was opened to reveal a table cloth (wonder of wonders), a thermos flask with steaming hot tea, not enamel mugs but porcelain cups and saucers, and slabs of lovely carrot cake, made by Mum that morning.

"Milk? Sugar?"

They might as well have been having afternoon tea at the Ritz. Kathy wouldn't have been surprised if there were cucumber sandwiches as well. The cake, of which Brian made short work, was delicious, and the tea was just the right thirst quencher for a warm day.

The flies were ever persistent, but they enjoyed their tea and chat until time to make a move. Promising to pick up a particular brand of hair conditioner that Mum wanted in town, she added that, plus a roll of fencing wire, to her requisition list.

"See you next week; thanks for the tea."

Kathy waved to her new friend through the window as they took off along the sun-baked strip and nosed the aircraft in the direction of their next port of call.

The week flew by, with each day different to the one before. Not all of Kathy's time was spent flying. Some days were 'on call' which meant that she had to be available should an unanticipated charter come in. It might be a passenger flight, a pick-up or a delivery, a bush fire spotting, or even search and rescue flights. Time spent on call was ideal for updating flight-related publications with the endless stream of amendments that arrived from the Department of Aviation.

The pilots were also responsible for washing the aircraft, and cleaning them inside. Kathy washed and polished with enthusiasm. If she had been told before that the job had domestic aspects, she might not have been so keen. She didn't care what she did. She revelled in the novelty of her new working day, whether flying, doing paperwork or hangar chores, or helping to fulfill the requisition orders sent in by stations and settlements. She had a lot to write about in her first letter home, and also to Pete.

She had visited an indigenous settlement, having her first contact with Aborigines who lived a tribal life to varying degrees. She discovered a totally different scenario to the urban environment in which she had grown up. There were no sealed roads, and many of the houses looked to be over-crowded and in disrepair. The children roamed in noisy groups, looking for entertainment. Always, they were followed by the camp dogs, a motley group of hounds of indiscriminate breed.

Listening, she had heard unfamiliar languages. It reminded her that another culture quite different to hers had existed in Australia all along. Some of the old people spoke very basic English, though their comprehension was more extensive. It had been a fascinating education.

"Can I pass you the dead horse?"

Glancing up, Kathy was surprised to see Mark, the chopper pilot, proffering a bottle of tomato sauce with a smile. *Why do people always speak to me when I have a mouth full?*

Swallowing, she wiped a dribble of juice from her chin with the back of her hand.

"Thanks," she managed at last "but you're a little late. I've almost finished."

"Well, would you like another sausage?" chimed in Chris. "You could have some tomato sauce then."

"Thanks, but no thanks. I've eaten more than enough already."

She was amused at their persistence. They were like a pair of shadows, presenting themselves in front of her shortly after she had arrived at the barbecue, wanting to get her a chair, a drink, something to nibble, perhaps another drink?

She glanced around, looking for Sarah, but her friend was on the far side of the garden, deep in conversation with people Kathy didn't know.

Later, she sidled past with a wink and a nudge saying, "Said you'd be popular, didn't I?" before disappearing into the crowd again.

Kathy rolled her eyes in exasperation. Sarah had made introductions when they had arrived, and some of the faces were familiar but she couldn't remember all the names. Except Mark and Chris of course. How could she forget them? They had a certain amount of charm, but they didn't give a girl a chance to catch her breath.

"Buzz off you two! You're as annoying as those motorized mosquitoes you try to fly. Let Kathy eat in peace." Brian detached himself from another discussion and clapped Mark on the shoulder.

"Ah, you're just trying to muscle in on the act yourself!" Chris grinned. "Look, you've got no show, mate. You've got to admit that flying rotary requires far more skill and intelligence than flying fixed wing, to say nothing of beauty, of course, as Kathy has no doubt noticed."

There were some good-natured jibes exchanged, and with no offense either given or taken, the two men wandered off in the direction of further drinks and convivial company.

"I thought I saw the hint of an appeal flit across your brow," said Brian.

"Brian, don't be silly! They're quite sweet really."

"Sweet! Somehow, I don't think they'd like to hear you say that. It sure isn't how I think of them."

Brian pulled up a chair beside her and straddled it, careful not to spill his beer in the process.

"So how was your first week?"

"I didn't know what to expect, but if I had expected anything at all, it would have been far from the reality."

"Is that good or bad?"

"Good. Don't worry, it's definitely good. It's such a different lifestyle, and I've seen so much that I can't believe I have been here only a week. I've enjoyed every minute. I made the right decision in coming here; I've no doubts at all about that."

The look he gave her was inscrutable, but he didn't comment.

***

With the beginning of the second week, Kathy had a better idea of what to expect. It didn't make her less nervous. This week she was on her own. With her unpacking done and the apartment now in order, she'd spent the Sunday evening reviewing her mud-maps and notes. Flight charts were spread out over the dining table, routes checked and tracks measured. She'd even made a list for herself of who she would find at each landing point, determined to remember the names.

Next morning, she surveyed herself in the mirror. The previous week had seen the development of a light tan which gave her a healthy glow. All the same, she applied a liberal application of sunscreen over her face. Some healthy sunshine was fine, but the leathery look was definitely out! A light dusting of powder, a touch of mascara, and she was ready.

Hurrying around to Brian's flat, she could see the sky was overcast. Still, the cloud base looked to be quite high, so it shouldn't interfere with her schedule.

She glared in mock annoyance at Brian as he scurried round the flat, shoes in one hand and the inevitable cup of coffee in the other. He didn't have Kathy's level of organization, and his last-minute panic to get ready was a regular event. She couldn't decide if his disorganization was exasperating, or reassuring in its consistency.

He got them to the office and then the airport on time, so she supposed this was the main thing. Today of all days, she didn't want to be late.

Her plane, for she was already starting to think of it as hers, was waiting on the tarmac outside the hanger, already fuelled for the day's flight. With solemn care, Kathy carried out the daily maintenance inspection, resisting the urge to do it twice for good measure. Everything was as it should be the first time.

"Where are you off to today, Kathy? Made up your mind yet? Perhaps we could give you a forecast for the South Pole, or the Gold Coast, or somewhere equally as exotic."

Kathy was a familiar face in the Briefing Office now, and had come to expect the early morning banter. They were not going to let her forget her first morning in a hurry.

"No? Oh well, I suppose it will have to be Area 85 as usual. Come and have a look at the charts. We'll see what sort of day we can give you."

The forecast was prepared, and would be in force for some hours yet, but as meteorological charts were updated on an ongoing basis, the staff sometimes gave an interim update. The Met Man now scratched his chin thoughtfully.

"Got your brolly with you? It looks like we're headed for a squall. Hard to say what time it will hit, but shouldn't be for a couple of hours yet. Anyway, on the route you're taking, you might even miss it altogether. I'd make a prompt start if I were you, and remember—keep out of those clouds."

Kathy needed no reminding on that score. Flying in clouds could leave you disorientated. They could hide unpleasant surprises, like hills and other physical structures. The impact could be terminal and that didn't fit with her long-term plans.

With the flight plan lodged, she hurried back to the plane. She had spurned all offers of help this morning, and had loaded the aircraft herself. This was her day, and no-one was going to interfere. With one final check that the load was adequately secured, she climbed into the cabin with a smile and a wave.

It felt like a first solo navigation exercise all over again. Easing the throttle forward until the aircraft began to roll, Kathy taxied to the run-up bay. Here she completed her pre-flight checks: mixture fully rich; fuel pump on; trim set for take-off; friction nut firm. Methodically, she checked all the gauges, the magnetos, and the aircraft controls. All being satisfactory, she pulled the side window closed, moved the door handle into the locked position, and taxied out to the holding point. She requested airways clearance, and took off.

The view over the MacDonnell Ranges was stunning. Kathy felt an unbelievable sense of freedom as she skimmed over the top. Their majesty took her breath away. Singing softly to herself with sheer pleasure, she completed some of the in-flight requirements of her flight plan, and settled down to monitor her progress. What had she been so nervous about?

She was soon at Arapunya Station. Circling the homestead once, she noted the vehicle moving out in a cloud of dust, then entered the downwind leg of the circuit area for the nearby strip which serviced the Station. By the time the utility had pulled up, with the usual dogs yapping in the back, she had landed and was unloading the mail and a few other bits and pieces.

"Hi! Got anything you want me to take back to town?"

"Just a few letters, love. The eldest is down in Adelaide at agricultural college, and we like to keep in regular contact. Never get to the big smoke much myself. Always seems a strange sort of place to me. All those people. A bloke could get himself lost down there."

The face beneath the dusty hat frowned in contemplation. Kathy suppressed a smile. City people would worry about getting lost in the bush, and here was a bushie contemplating the horrors of being lost in the city!

They exchanged further pleasantries, and the inevitable chat about the weather.

"Don't like the look of that sky. Can't say for sure, but we might have a bad one coming on. Mind you, we could do with some rain."

Agreeing it would probably be a good thing, Kathy had the uncomfortable feeling that the sky was closing in a little. Not wanting to linger, she took the outgoing mail, bade farewell and set course for Mulga Downs.

She found it eerie when the environment around her changed so quickly. The gathering clouds cast shadows making navigating a challenge, and a light turbulence buffeted the aircraft. The first few drops of rain hit the windscreen, and dispersed in star-shaped patterns.

At least, they did for a while. The rain steadily increased, until it seemed she had hit a wall of water, and torrents poured over the windscreen obscuring visibility. She could hardly see anywhere but down. She felt isolated and alone, cut-off from the outside world.

Carefully, she checked the controls. If the rain didn't ease off soon, she was going to be in a sticky situation. Her eyes scanned the instrument panel constantly, ensuring she was maintaining height and heading. Looking at the time, Kathy calculated she should be almost there. She peered out, trying to reconcile what she could see with her mud-map. Miraculously, the grey curtain parted in front of the windscreen, and there was a lull in the storm.

She spied a cluster of buildings, right on track. What a relief! Giving a routine 'All Stations' broadcast to any planes that might be in the circuit area of Mulga Downs that she was in-bound, Kathy was startled to have an acknowledgement from not one but two aircraft that were somewhere ahead of her and preparing to land. She scanned the horizon, cautious about entering the circuit pattern until she had the other aircraft sighted. A sudden movement caught her eye, and she stared harder. She spotted it again. Good grief! A chopper was barely discernible against the mottled background of the tableau below, and following behind was another.

As Kathy watched they landed in turn, and a station wagon moved towards them. She lowered the under carriage, feeling the reassuring clunk as the wheels locked into position. Easing back on power, she lowered the flaps and prepared for landing. The wheels connected smoothly with the surface, and she kept to the middle of the dirt strip in her landing roll, mindful of the possible dangers in soft, slushy edges.

She taxied up to the other two machines, pulled on the handbrake, and cut the engine. Grimacing as the rain hit her face, Kathy swung herself out of the cabin and opened the door to the luggage compartment. As she reached for the mail bag, she heard footsteps approaching from behind her.

"You'd better hurry it up unless you want that delicate hair of yours to go all frizzy."

Astonished, Kathy swung around, ignoring the rain sending rivulets down her face, and leaving wet patches on her blouse.

Her heart sank; the man from the Briefing Office. Why was he here?

He hadn't been around last week when she had flown in with Brian. His face was shielded from the rain by the wide brimmed hat he wore but it didn't hide the piercing eyes that regarded her, nor the look of bemusement. The look sent a quiver down her spine. Conscious she was now getting very wet, Kathy felt a surge of irritation.

"If you could make yourself useful instead of standing around, I might get the deliveries unloaded, and get back in out of this rain. I've got a box of stores to go."

She turned back to the luggage compartment to find the box.

"I don't think you're going anywhere for a while, except into the back of that car. The rain has set in for now; you'd best be staying put."

To add emphasis to his words, the rain suddenly changed from a light fall to a raging torrent. He grabbed the box of stores and made a dash for the car. Kathy hovered uncertainly, seeking temporary and largely ineffectual shelter under the wing. She had no desire to go anywhere with him. If only she knew how long this weather was going to last. A glance skyward was not reassuring. If anything, the horizon appeared darker than ever.

"Look, you can stay there and drown for all I care, but you're expected up at the house for lunch. You can drive with me, or you can run along behind. Take your pick!"

Rude bugger! From all she had heard about Alex Woodleigh and his low tolerance for those who didn't measure up, Kathy was surprised he employed a man like that. It seemed she didn't have much choice. Grasping the bag of mail and her backpack, blinking as needle-like shafts of rain stung her eyes, Kathy ran for the car. As she approached, the back door was flung open. Clambering in, and slamming the door behind her, she looked around at the other occupants. She couldn't believe her luck. With the landing and her reception, she had forgotten about the two choppers that had come in ahead of her. Chris and Mark sat there, grinning at her.

"It's amazing who you meet on a rainy day, isn't it?" said Chris archly. "Not a bad landing, Kathy, especially given the weather. I suppose you do good landings all the time."

There was a snort from the driver's seat, as their taciturn chauffeur put the car into gear and slowly turned around, heading back towards the homestead. Mark turned from the front passenger's seat, and pulled a long face at them both. Kathy stifled a giggle, and didn't dare look at either of them, for fear of laughing outright.

Looking up, her eyes met those of the driver in his rear vision mirror. He was watching her, and his disdain was clearly visible. Her humour disappeared. At least with Chris and Mark there, she avoided the necessity for any conversation with him.

Presumably he was a station hand, and so was unlikely to be joining them at the homestead for lunch. Perhaps Mr. Woodleigh would take them back to the airstrip when the weather cleared.

She settled back in her seat, answering the questions that were flung at her and trying at the same time to take in some of the passing scenery. She was careful not to look in the mirror again.

The homestead sat like an oasis in the surrounding countryside. Painted a cool white, with enclosed verandas on all sides except for the front, it nestled in the middle of extensive lawns. Kathy could just make out the rose garden, and established trees but with the obscured vision, wasn't able to identify the varieties. It looked well-kept.

The whole effect must have been achieved with bore water. The salinity level was presumably fairly low. The rainwater tanks that she could see would service the needs of the house. They pulled up outside a small gate. As she opened the car door, Kathy could hear the whirring noise made by the wind vein on the water tower near the fence surrounding the homestead and garden.

With no instructions other than, "Okay, make a run for it," the three passengers dived out of the car doors, and ran through the gate to the shelter of the veranda. Kathy had grabbed her backpack and the mail bag before leaving the car, and clutched it tight in a vain effort to protect it from the rain.

As they wiped their feet on an expansive door mat, an inner door opened and a small white-haired woman stepped through. Surprisingly for someone living in this climate, her skin was a flawless alabaster, though still featuring fine laughter lines. Her white hair was not an indication of infirmity, for she moved sprightly, and regarded them with interest.

"This is the lot. All came in together, more or less." Their driver had followed them. "Just going over to the sheds to check how the roof's holding up. I'll bring the stores in out of the car when I come back."

"All right," the woman responded. "Come in the rest of you. Nasty weather to be caught out in. Still, it will mean that the dams and tanks are replenished again, and for that I am thankful. I assume you're all hungry?"

She led the way into the hall, wide in structure and featuring family photos above the mid-height timber panelling and gestured to a door leading to one side.

You boys can wash up through there if you like, and perhaps the young lady would like to come with me. There's another bathroom off my bedroom you can use."

"Thank you," said Kathy, as she followed her hostess. "This is most unexpected. It's very much appreciated, but you don't need to go to all this trouble."

"Nonsense, my dear. Kathy, isn't it? I'm Rose Woodleigh. I've been on the radio to Bert from Arapunya, and he said you were on your way. I heard also from the Morris's that they are awash, and their strip is no longer safe to land on, so that's one stop you won't have to make today."

Kathy laughed inwardly. With the effectiveness of the grapevine in this community, it would be difficult to keep any secrets.

"You can't go anywhere in this rain," continued Rose, "so you might as well wait in comfort. The boys are doing some aerial mustering for us, and they can't be out in this sort of weather either. They were operating close by so we got on the radio, and told them to come back too."

The room Rose led her into delighted Kathy. The light and airy room featured shades of delicate pink and cream throughout, with French doors opening out onto the enclosed veranda. A comfortable-looking chair was positioned close to the doors, presumably to capture the natural light. It looked a good place for reading. The upholstery, bedspread and the curtains all utilised an attractive full-blown rose pattern. Thinking the room could easily have been featured in the pages of a furnishing magazine, Kathy wondered if Rose Woodleigh had an affinity for roses because of her name, or if that was merely coincidental. Perhaps Rose was also the architect of the rose garden.

The colour scheme was carried through into the ensuite bathroom. Rose gave her a fresh towel, and departed to check on the lunch.

"Just come through to the dining room when you are finished, dear."

Kathy couldn't resist a smile when she realised that the soap was rose scented too. Loosening her hair, she briefly towelled it in an attempt to dry it a little. That rotten man was right. Her hair fanned out in a frizzy halo! A hair dryer sat on the vanity bench. Being sure that her hostess would not mind if she borrowed it, she felt a certain snug satisfaction in being able to restore her hair to its former sleek and shining glory. She took longer than she meant to, but on impulse, she quickly washed her face and applied a little lipstick. Backpacks came in handy sometimes! They carried a variety of treasures.

She paused uncertainly in the hallway. Where was the dining room? Hearing a burst of laughter, and a pair of familiar voices, she headed in that direction. Never slow when there was food around, Mark and Chris were already seated at the table.

"Too late, slow coach, we've eaten yours." Mark grinned, barely suppressing his humour. In response, he received a look of admonishment from Rose.

"Of course, they haven't eaten yours. Even if they had, there is more than enough to go around, and for seconds as well."

She indicated to Kathy where she should sit at the table.

"Find everything you needed? So pleasant to be able to freshen up, isn't it?"

"Oh, Kathy always looks nice—certainly the best-looking pilot I know!" said Chris with a wink in her direction.

A new voice broke in. "Well, she's got you two under control already, that's for sure."

Kathy's blush deepened. She hadn't heard him come in behind her but she picked up the same scent she'd first noticed in the briefing office. Surely, he should knock or something?

"Now Alex, there's nothing wrong with young men appreciating an attractive young woman. Many appreciated me in my day and I found absolutely nothing wrong with it. Hurry up and sit down, and I'll start serving."

"Not so much of the 'my day' Rose", said Mark. "We still appreciate you, and always will."

Kathy felt such an idiot. She should have known his self-assurance indicated he was more than just a station hand. No wonder Rose treated him with such familiarity. She decided to ignore him, even though he was sitting at the head of the table and immediately to her right.

She was surprisingly hungry, and turned her attention to the lunch. Hot pumpkin soup with crusty home-made bread, and followed by quiche and salad.

"Who's for some apple pie?" inquired Rose.

As far as the men were concerned, the question was a no-brainer, but Kathy passed with regret.

"It looks and smells wonderful but I've had enough already," she said. "I shouldn't have had so much of that bread but it was so tasty. I'd love a coffee if that's on offer."

"Ah Kathy," sighed Mark. "You don't know what you're missing." True to his earlier promise, he tucked into Kathy's share as well as his own.

With the serious business of eating out of the way, the conversation picked up its pace. Chris and Mark described their morning's work to Alex, and they discussed how best to tackle the remaining areas to be covered. Kathy found her attention diverted by Rose. Like Mum Gardner, she seemed eager for some feminine company. Kathy had to describe in detail how she came to be flying, what brought her to Alice, what her family thought of it all, and what her impressions of the Centre were.

"Of course, I'd already heard a little about you. News travels fast up here."

What sort of news had Rose heard? Probably her precious son had come home and told her about the 'incompetent pilot-come-husband-hunter' that he'd encountered in the briefing office. How could such a lovely and hospitable woman have given birth to such a rude and arrogant son? She surveyed him surreptitiously, relying on her long eyelashes to shield her gaze. Sarah had said he was good looking. She supposed he was, in a rugged sort of way—if you liked the type, and she definitely didn't.

His broad shoulders and strong hands were an indication he could tackle the heavy work load required around the station. There was a determined set to his jaw line, his face masked by heavy eyebrows. He looked like a man who was accustomed to getting his own way. She flushed suddenly as those same eyebrows were lifted sardonically. He had been aware of her perusal, and a cynical smile pulled at the corner of his mouth.

She quickly looked away. *With his natural arrogance, he probably thinks I am interested in him as well as every other man this side of the black stump. Well, I've got news for him, and none of it good!*

"Kathy," queried Mark. "Are you going to the races next week?"

"I don't think so. Should I be? I've seen the race course on the way out to the airport, but I don't have plans to go to any race meetings. To be honest, I don't know much about the sport."

"I'm talking about the Hart's Range races. Hasn't anyone told you? It's a three-day picnic meeting out at Hart's Range. The track isn't far from Plenty River Station, about a hundred and eighty kilometres from town."

Kathy was incredulous. "You expect me to drive a hundred and eighty kilometres, just to go to the races? Where do the horses come from, and where does everybody stay? I didn't think there was a motel out that way?"

Chris laughed. "Everybody goes. It's a mixture of town and country. There are the people from the properties round about, and of course lots of people drive out from town. The horses are trucked in mostly from Alice and Tennant Creek, but some are from further afield."

"You haven't answered the lady's most important question," said Alex dryly.

Chris raised his eyebrows in query.

"Where is she going to stay? You're right; there isn't a motel. There are a couple of corrugated iron sheds that have

54

basic shower and toilet facilities, but otherwise everybody camps out. Too primitive for a city slicker, I should think. What with the flies and the dust, it wouldn't be your cup of tea."

Kathy bristled.

"What you think, Mr. Woodleigh, is irrelevant. I may come from the city, but I'm no stranger to camping."

"Call me Alex, please. We don't stand on formality here." He couldn't have been more sarcastic if he tried. "This is different to your Girl Guide excursions."

"Now Alex, don't make assumptions about people, and stop teasing Kathy." Rose Woodleigh started clearing things from the table.

"Actually," she said to Kathy. "You'd probably quite enjoy it. It's a friendly atmosphere, like a carnival really and it's more than just racing. There are all sorts of races and competitions for the kiddies, and some for the adults too. Some people go just on the second or third day. That's when the most important races are run, and of course there's the ball in the evening."

"Ball? You mean a dance? Out there in the bush? If there are no facilities, where is it held?"

Mark chimed in at this point.

"There's a big shed, built especially for that purpose. It has a bar, and even a stage for the band. The musicians usually come out from Alice. It's a great night. People disappear into their tents after the last race, and emerge all done up to the nines. Everyone dances, even those who can't. You've got to go to a picnic race meeting at least once in your life.

He eyed off the last slice of pie, but with a sigh, left it in the dish. He turned back to Kathy.

"I tell you what—I'll drive you out there if you like."

"What, in that heap you call a car?" hooted Chris. "You'd never make it. Kathy, if you'd like to get there, and back again, you had better travel in style and come with me."

"Hey, one step at a time. I haven't even said that I'll go yet. It sounds like an experience, but I'll have to check my roster. I couldn't go for the whole three days, but perhaps as Rose suggests, I could go for the last day. I'll let you know through the week, and I'll sort out transport options after that."

Privately, she thought perhaps Sarah would like to go as well, and they could share petrol expenses and drive up together. It might be more diplomatic.

"I hate to interrupt this cozy chat, but the rain stopped some time ago. I'd better take you back to the strip."

Alex pushed his chair back and stood up. The others followed suit, the two men with a trace of reluctance, and Kathy with a feeling of guilt. She had been so engrossed in the conversation, that she hadn't noticed the drumming on the roof had quietened. She would have to give her tail feathers a shake to make up for lost time. At least she didn't have to worry about stopping off at the Morris's. Perhaps some of the other strips would be unserviceable because of the rain as well. She would examine them with care before attempting a landing.

She extended her thanks to Rose for the unexpected lunch, and hurried after the others. Already the sun was shining through a gap in the clouds. The air smelt fresh, and the grass and trees looked cleaner with all the dust washed off.

The drive back to the strip was slow, as numerous large puddles had to be avoided, or forded with care. The three machines, the last droplets drying in the emerging sun, sat quietly waiting. With a surge of affection for her white and yellow plane, Kathy suddenly couldn't wait to be inside and away.

Alex remained silent throughout the drive. He pulled up close to all machines, and engaged in some last-minute discussion with Mark and Chris about the areas in which they were to be working that afternoon.

Kathy got out without a word, and busied herself with checking the fuel tanks for water, in case any had leaked in during the storm. She was examining the fuel sample that she had drained off from the bottom of the tanks, when Alex wandered over. She sensed him coming, as much as heard him. Her antenna was becoming more sensitive to his presence.

"Well, I can see you don't waste much time. You've those two dancing on a string already. If you continue with this rate of success, you won't have to worry about getting your hands dirty with flying for too long."

"My name is Kathy, or Miss Sullivan to you. Sorry to disappoint, but you'll have to put up with me for a while yet. When I undertake a job, I stick at it."

She emptied out the fuel sample and tucked the container in the door pocket. Turning back to Alex, she was dismissive.

"At least I'm not tied to my mother's apron strings, not like some people I could mention."

She regretted the jibe as soon as she had made it. The comment was juvenile and made unfair inferences about Rose Woodleigh. If she wanted a reaction, she got it.

"Miaow! Keep your claws in around me or I might clip them for you. Next time, I'll leave you out here to drown."

Those eyes raked her derisively, speaking volumes before she looked away, confused by the unexpected frisson that rippled through her. He spun around, and stormed back to the car. Kathy watched him briefly before climbing into the aircraft. At least she had got in a punch, and there was some satisfaction in that.

CHAPTER 4

THE WEEK PASSED in a haze of take-offs, landings, cups of tea with so many new names and faces to learn. Some days Kathy thought she was getting to know her way around and what she was doing and then something would happen to make her aware just how vast the country was. Being the new girl on the block, she came in for plenty of teasing, but she took it with the good nature in which it was intended, even if it did exasperate her.

She looked forward to debriefing with her colleagues each evening. Some of her trips were still with Brian, or one of the other pilots, and driving home from the airport with him gave her the opportunity to de-brief on the technical aspects of her day.

Sarah was more interested in the news Kathy brought back, and what was happening on all the stations and outposts. If anyone thought by moving to the back of beyond, they were blending into the background, they'd be sadly mistaken. The grapevine thrived in the region and news of each person and what they were up to travelled fast.

Sarah raised the issue of the Harts Range race meeting early in the week.

"Kathy, you'll have to come. It's too good an opportunity to miss. You'll get to meet every one who's on your regular mail runs, and a lot of other people as well. It's not often they all come together like this and it'll be an experience for you." She raised her eyebrows in query. "Have you got something you can wear to the ball? This is a dress-up affair you know."

"I'm rostered on for this Saturday, but as luck has it, I'm free for the rest of the weekend. I've got the holiday Monday off, no joy flights or anything. Isn't that great?" She paused, with a frown reflecting her deliberations at the proposal. The clothing was yet another issue.

"That gives us the Sunday and the Monday. Won't it be too far to travel for only two days? I'd feel guilty if you didn't go on the Saturday and waited just for me. You've really been looking forward to this."

"It's not a problem—really. The first day is the quietest anyway as lots of people don't arrive that early. Sunday is when all the fun really starts. It would be silly of either of us to go on our own. Much better driving together."

"Well, if you're really sure…"

"Great. That's settled. Chris and Mark are going too so we can meet up with them. If they get there first, they can reserve a quiet camping spot. Did I tell you who else would be there?"

Sarah swept any objections away with a swirl of chatter. Kathy listened, but at the same time mentally ran through her wardrobe. What to wear to this ball? That was a problem.

When she had packed for her new job, the last thing that she considered was evening wear. There were dress shops in town though, and Sarah led her through them, one by one, critically assessing the assortment on the racks. There was only one thing that approached the satisfaction of buying new clothes for oneself, and that was buying new clothes for someone else. Sarah took on the task with regimented delight.

"I think that green suits you quite well. Give this one a try." The dress that she held up had shoestring straps, a low-slung back and a mid-calf handkerchief hem. It joined a couple of others that were slung over her arm.

"It's a lovely colour," Kathy agreed. "But I'm not sure about the style. That's a cocktail length, isn't it? It doesn't really measure up as a ball gown."

"Well, this isn't a conventional sort of ball. I mean... calling it a ball is rather tongue-in-cheek. It's a bush dance really and believe me, in that dress you'll slay 'em. Try it on."

Kathy acquiesced, and tried others too but in the end came back to the green. There was something about the cut and the way it draped that made her feel good. She sucked in her stomach and turned this way and that in front of the mirror until Sarah told her to stop being so silly and just buy it. She did. She packed the dress and strappy shoes along with her jeans, check shirt, boots, hat and sunglasses for the drive to Hart's Range.

They made the journey in Gordon, Sarah's station wagon. Driving over the dusty roads provided a totally different experience to a quick and easy flight. Sarah put together a collection of cassettes they could listen to along the way, and they sang along to their favourite tracks. Kathy was in charge of the music while Sarah drove.

They pulled off the road into a short lay-by for a mid-morning break. The cloud of dust stirred up in their wake hung heavily in the air, shielding the road behind them. They had long since left the bitumen behind. As she swatted the flies competing for her morning tea, Kathy scanned the horizon. They were a long way from anywhere. A silence that enveloped them, though as she listened, there were small noises from flies and the inevitable caw-caw of the crows. She shivered, glad she wasn't travelling alone.

"Come on," Sarah said as she screwed the lid back on the thermos. "Let's get moving. If we make good time, we should be there by midday."

They packed up, had a final stretch and climbed back into Gordon. They passed the turn-off to Plenty River Station.

"That means there's not much further to go," advised Sarah. "I'm looking forward to today's events."

She had barely spoken before there was a bang. The car slewed alarmingly on the loose surface. Sarah fought to bring it under directional control as it skidded dangerously close to the white posts at the side of the road. Kathy braced herself against the dashboard, expecting any minute that they might come to grief. They didn't. Sarah managed to keep the car on the road and slowed to a stop.

Climbing out, they could see what the problem was. The front passenger tyre was shredded, no doubt having come to grief on a sharp stone.

"Damn!" exclaimed Sarah. "Just as well I checked the spare before we left. The only catch is that the storage well for the tyre is in the back—under all the luggage!"

"That's okay. It won't take us long to unload and then reload again. We didn't bring too much with us. Where do you keep the jack?"

Kathy opened the rear door and started hauling everything out from the rear compartment. "You're a good driver, Sarah. We could easily have come to grief, given the speed at which we were travelling."

"I had my doubts for a while. I thought we were going to end up in the scrub at the very least." Sarah still looked shaken.

Together, they lifted the tyre from the well and the jack also. Then they struck a new problem. The wheel nuts were immovable.

Kathy strained against the wheel brace. Strands of hair were plastered to her forehead and she wiped off the perspiration with the back of her sleeve. She was just about to ask what Plan B was, when a cloud of dust down the road indicated they would shortly have company. Through the haze, they sighted a Land Cruiser, which slowed and drew up behind them.

"Great. I hope whoever it is has a big set of muscles!" Sarah moved to greet the newcomers. A well-groomed young woman got out of the driver's seat. Her vehicle must have been air-conditioned, as she looked cool and composed making Kathy feel gritty and dishevelled by comparison. Damn. Another woman. She won't be much use and with those fingernails she doesn't look as though she's about to try.

The passenger door slammed, drawing Kathy's attention. She gaped in astonishment at the man now standing beside it. Alex Woodleigh.

She chewed her lip in annoyance as Sarah moved to greet them, explaining what had happened—as if it wasn't obvious.

She knew her response was childish but even so, she grasped the wheel brace and had one more attempt to loosen the nuts, grunting with the effort.

She heard his footsteps on the loose surface before a pair of dusty boots entered her peripheral vision.

"If you care to stand aside, I'll get on with it."

She stood up reluctantly, nearly jumping as his hand brushed against hers. He was standing too close, almost making contact unavoidable. It felt like a burn mark on the back of her hand.

His manner was brusque, and he didn't even look at Kathy as he bent down and applied himself to the task. For a while, nothing happened and she felt a fleeting moment of satisfaction before slowly, slowly, each nut began to move and was soon spinning on its bolt. That done, he wound up the jack and eased the tyre from its supports.

"If you stand back, I'll have more room to work." Alex replaced the damaged tyre with the spare, secured it firmly and released the jack. He then heaved the shredded tyre back into the storage well before standing back and brushing the dirt from his hands on the side of his jeans.

"Ladies—I'll let you re-pack your luggage. You know where everything goes."

"Thanks so much, Alex" Sarah said. "We would have been here for ages if you hadn't come along."

"Well, someone else would have come past soon, so we wouldn't have been without help for long." Kathy sounded churlish, even to herself. "Thanks anyway."

"My pleasure," he drawled. "Can't imagine you've had to change many tyres on your own."

Kathy looked up to find that her glare was met by a look of bemusement. She wasn't sure how to react. Was he sneering or merely teasing? Probably the former.

"Alex? If you're finished, we should be going. We've lost enough time already."

The driver of the other vehicle didn't wait for a response but headed back to the Land Cruiser. She'd not entered into any exchange with the other two women and clearly had no interest in their predicament.

"Good to see you've got a competent driver at the wheel." Kathy smiled with saccharine sweetness. She got no response other than a grunt. *Score for me,* she thought.

With a nod to Sarah, Alex turned and swung himself into their vehicle. It eased back onto the road and accelerated, coating Kathy and Sarah in a fine layer of dust. Neither of the car's occupants looked back.

"What an interesting exchange," said Sarah. "You two aren't exactly friendly, are you? Something happened that you haven't told me about?"

"Nothing at all." Kathy was abrupt. "He's arrogant and obnoxious, that's all. I've struck his type before. Usually, their behaviour covers up their own inadequacies. Pity he's such a moron, as his mother is quite lovely."

"You're right about Rose," Sarah agreed. "There were sparks between you two though. Perhaps," she added with devilment, "it's a case of opposites attract!" She wisely desisted from making further comment.

"The driver was Melissa Gilbert, by the way. Friendly soul, isn't she? Her father has the station at Plenty River—we just passed the turnoff—so they'll definitely be at the races. No need to camp out in tents for that lot."

The day was event-filled, as had been promised. Vehicles filled the parking area by the time they arrived, and utilities and four-wheeled drives seemed to be the order of the day. There were people and dogs and horse floats and of course, the bookies. What was a race meeting without the betting? Kathy was wide-eyed as she took it all in, but there were other matters to attend to first, like finding a shady place to park and a relatively quiet and private place in which to pitch their tent. Not too far from the facilities though.

Chris and Mark soon spotted the two women, and guided them to an area that they had marked out and reserved the day before. It seemed to meet their requirements and they pitched the tent and made camp. They had a pop-up gazebo, folding table and chairs and a small gas-fired camping stove. It soon looked like 'home'. Their dresses were sheathed in protective plastic, and were hung from a supporting rail for the gazebo so the creases could drop out. All organized. That left them free to explore.

The smell of sizzling sausages drew them to the catering area and signalled lunch time. The organizing committee had done well, and in an open-sided shed, a couple of barbeques were in operation, providing the usual sausages, chicken kebabs and meat patties. Bowls of salad were laid out on trestle tables. Some people jammed a sausage or two, squirted with tomato sauce between a couple of slices of bread and headed back to the action and others took the more laid-back option and sat at the picnic tables with a platter of selected meats and salads.

They surveyed the options, standing clear of the milling crowd. There were a few familiar faces and Kathy nodded to those. She saw Alex and Melissa seated at one of the tables with a couple of friends. They were laughing, and as she watched, Melissa placed her hand on his arm in a familiar gesture.

"Over here—I think there are some free tables this way."

She led them to a table on the other side of the lunch area. She preferred to avoid the man, rather than ignore him. Why put yourself in the path of unpleasantness?

"I am so hungry," exclaimed Sarah. "I vote we sit-down to eat. We can wander around later."

"Sounds like a plan," agreed Kathy. "I'm happy to relax and unwind for a while. Not that I've been doing much—you did all the driving."

"Don't you want to see what's happening around the track?" queried Mark plaintively. You'll miss out on everything if you sit here all day."

"Don't let us stop you," said Sarah. "We want a restful lunch, that's all. If you two want to get back to the track, that's fine. We'll join you shortly."

"No, we'll keep you company. Tell you what, Chris, I'll get us some sausages." He returned with the divine smelling sausages and fried onion smothered with sauce, which were scoffed with enthusiasm. The two men regaled the women with detail on who was already there and what had happened since their arrival. They had borrowed the company helicopter on the proviso that they paid for fuel, and had flown to the site the previous day. Their camp only consisted of a couple of swags, which was just as well as a mustering chopper was small and not practical for carting luggage. The advantage lay in putting people down near the action though. Their chatter was entertaining but soon the women took pity on them and followed them out into the bright sunshine.

The next race was due in twenty minutes, so they made their way first to the saddling yards to cast non-expert eyes over the starters. The horses were led around the small enclosure or trotted gently as part of a warm-up process.

"I like the look of that horse. What do you think?" Sarah pointed out a glossy chestnut that pranced and danced sideways against the restraining attempts of its rider. "She looks ready to go now!"

Kathy was not so sure. "It might be over too quickly with her. What about the quiet one over there—the black horse? He might be conserving his strength. The jockey's wearing a green similar to the colour of my dress as well. That's got to be a good sign."

Chris was exasperated. "Don't you two know anything about anything? You have to study a horse's form. The colours the jockey is wearing have no bearing at all. Look, I happen to have it on good authority that number five is a sure thing. I'm going to put my money on that one."

"Sure thing? There is no such thing as a sure thing." Kathy was certain of that if nothing else.

Chris was right though. When it came to horses and racing, she had no idea. Her exposure to racing had not extended beyond watching the Melbourne Cup each year on television. She had never attended a race meeting before.

Mark came to her rescue and explained the intricacies of placing a bet as he led her over to the row of bookies. She could go for a win, or bet on a place or, if she was brave, nominate a trifecta. Kathy was certain she would lose her money, but it didn't matter really. New experiences were part of the fun. After appropriate tutelage, she approached one of the bookies and placed her bet, as did Sarah and Chris.

She saw Alex also placing a bet, while Melissa waited nearby. The woman had that air of assurance that said, 'This is my domain and I'm at home here.' She was stylishly turned out, though still in keeping with the character of the event. Kathy was sure Melissa had seen them, but the woman gave them no acknowledgement, greeting others instead.

Kathy turned back to her own party, still debating their choices.

"Come on Mark," said Sarah. "Which horse are you backing?

In spite of his more expert knowledge, Mark declined with a grin.

"I try to pick the winner just for fun and that is enough for me. I like the money in my pocket and that's where it's going to stay, not financing the lifestyle of some bush bookie!"

They teased him good naturedly about not entering into the spirit of things, but mostly because they just enjoyed teasing. As it turned out, each of them picked a different horse to win. Kathy felt confident that one of them would be richer by the end of the race because being a bush meeting, there were not many starters anyway.

The horses were led out to the starting gate and people were enticed away from the beer tent and other areas of shade to prop themselves against the railing. The race caller climbed the ladder to a small cabin set on poles to the side of the track, ready to give the punters a running description of the riders and their mounts. There was the inevitable jostling at the gate. The horses all knew what was coming and were as keyed up as the jockeys. The starter's gun sounded and they were off. They couldn't see what was happening at the far side of the track, but as the horses entered the straight and neared the winning post, the crowd whooped and yelled. They thundered past with a cloud of dust and the winning rider pumping his fist in the air.

Kathy was right that one of them would pick the winning horse. Mark was the best judge of horse flesh, so neither he nor any of the others were any richer—except that Mark was the only one who hadn't lost anything. They took their loss with good grace and moved on, pausing here and there to catch up with a familiar face or perhaps to be introduced to someone new.

She saw Alex approach the bookies after the race to collect his winnings, so he must have made a more informed choice. *Bully for you.*

Between races, there were other events for two-legged rather than four-legged contestants. Guys in their utes drove an obstacle course. There were piggy-back races with the men carrying women on their backs. Even the kids got in on the act with an old-fashioned sack race and then an egg-and-spoon race.

There was a rolling pin throwing competition for the women. Kathy declined to participate, feeling that, giving the women the rolling pins to play with whilst the men got to drive the utes was sexist, but she still laughed at the antics and yelled encouragement with the best of them. When it came to the piggy-back race, even Kathy couldn't hold out.

"C'mon Kathy! It'll be such a lark. You're lighter than me so Chris had better carry you and Mark can carry me." Sarah was bossy, in a cheerful sort of way.

"I'm not sure this is really my thing," Kathy grumbled.

"Just get on," said Chris. "Gosh, you're only a lightweight. The two of us are bound to win."

"Don't be so sure," answered Mark. "I think Sarah's wearing spurs so I'll probably go a million miles an hour!"

They lined up at the starting line, with Kathy still feeling self-conscious and Sarah goading them all on. There was a field of around twelve starters and good-natured jibing came from all sides. They all attracted attention and the race-caller in the tower even got into the spirit of things. The flag dropped and they were off, with Sarah attempting to push and shove any other couple that came too close to her and Mark. It seemed anything went in this sort of race. In spite of that, Chris and Kathy really did pull to the head of the pack, and she couldn't help but get excited—keeping an eye on Sarah of course.

Perhaps Chris was watching them too instead of looking where he was going as suddenly, he stumbled on a tuft of grass, nearly losing his balance. He soon recovered but another couple swept past them to claim first place. Chris and Kathy were second and Mark and Sarah came in third with the men panting from their exertions.

Flushed and jubilant, Kathy slid from Chris's back, calling out to Sarah that she and Chris had beat them at least. Straightening up, she found herself looking straight into the eyes of Alex Woodleigh. He was standing with Melissa Gilbert at the winning line. He must have been watching her. He gave her a hard-faced and enigmatic look, which had the effect of flattening the moment. He certainly hadn't been cheering her on. She hastily looked away and made sure not to look in his direction again.

The daytime events finished up shortly before five o'clock, and everyone drifted off to their individual campsites to clean-up for the ball that evening.

"What a great day," said Sarah. "I haven't had so much fun in ages."

Kathy noted the glance that Chris and Mark exchanged, though neither said anything.

Come on," Sarah continued. "Let's make a dash for the showers and get in before the crowd. Who knows how long the hot water will last?"

"Good thinking. I'd love to wash my hair too. Do you think there will be a power point for the hair dryer?" There was, and plenty of hot water, thanks to the solar unit on the roof.

With deference to the demand from others, their showers were super quick. The interior of the shed was transformed as women primped and preened, and effected the change from dusty to dazzling. There was plenty of light-hearted chat, conscious all the time that the sound carried and the men in the facility next door could hear most of what was said.

With the shower and shampoo under control, hair dried and coiffed, and make-up applied, Sarah and Kathy slipped back to their camp. Here they retrieved their dresses and slipped them on, also exchanging their practical footwear for evening shoes, strappier and more appropriate for dancing.

They admired each other, and declared themselves ready. There was still time before the ball was to start. They had anticipated this before leaving town, and had brought a range of canapés and nibbles with them, and also had a bottle of champagne in the cooler. Chris and Mark were to join them for pre-dance refreshments.

A wolf whistle pierced the air as the men made their way over to the tent.

"Well... don't you two scrub up a treat!" Chris whistled his appreciation.

Not to be outdone, Mark repeated, "Very nice, very nice."

The two men had clearly been through the tin-shed shower as well, and looked ready for some social action. Mark did the honours with the champagne cork, and the four friends raised glasses in a toast, before settling on the camp chairs and admiring the morphing colours of the encroaching evening.

The cooling temperature and changing light brought a stillness over the landscape. The sounds of the bush changed, as the day creatures grew quiet and those of the night stretched and got ready for nocturnal explorations.

A rumbling background of diesel generators dotted around the camp ground was overlaid by the voices that carried on the night air. Mostly, those noises faded into insignificance alongside of the natural sounds of the night birds and occasional howl of a dingo or snicker of a horse.

The sky faded to twilight by the time they made their way across the camp ground and into the harsh light of the entertainment area. People drifted in from all directions. They were hardly recognisable as the race-attendees from earlier in the day. Everyone had made a special effort to wash off the dust and get spruced up. Even the main shed had received a make-over. Coloured light globes were in place and a band, having driven up from Alice, warmed up at the far end.

"G'day Kath!" boomed a voice. Tom Daly from Jinka grinned at her in welcome. "I reckon this dance is mine."

Tom issued a statement rather than an invitation. Kathy acquiesced and he swept her onto the dance floor. At times it seemed the tin roof was about to lift off with the combined noise of the band, and the general revelry. Young and old, everyone gave every indication of enjoying themselves. Would-be dancers cut in on other couples with a tap on the shoulder and so Kathy often found herself with a different partner by the end of a song. Chaos reigned.

She had no shortage of dance partners. She didn't expect though to suddenly find herself in the arms of Alex Woodleigh. How on earth did that happen? Before she could reflect further, he swung her first this way and then that, resulting in her spinning back and into his arms. She would have pulled away but he held her in a firm grip, the hand in the small of her back pressing her closely to him. She could feel the heat of his body and was aware of the muscular strength that enveloped her. He was so close that she could breathe in his scent, a musky man scent that was strangely appealing.

As her eyes moved upwards, she took in the smattering of chest hairs that curled at the top of his open-necked shirt and she was acutely aware she was dancing with the epitome of finely-tuned masculinity. Lingering briefly on the patch of skin that was directly in front of her, she shifted her gaze higher and reddened as she saw that he was watching her. The slightly raised eyebrow wordlessly asked if she liked what she was seeing. She flushed and pushed him away.

"I've got a headache. I need to sit down."

He didn't object and hadn't spoken a single word to her in the entire encounter but Kathy was sure she could feel his eyes on her as she pushed through the crowd of dancers to the collection of tables and chairs. She welcomed the chance to sit out the rest of the bracket and the next, as it gave her an opportunity to look around. She also needed to process what had just happened between her and Alex.

She had known he would be at the races, but hadn't expected to have any interaction with him. She especially didn't expect what she had just experienced. It couldn't be attraction. He wasn't the sort of man who appealed to her. Why then did she feel like a dizzy teenager, just from being in his arms?

Dismissing ludicrous thoughts, she turned her attention back to the action on the dance floor. It didn't matter whether people had a partner or not. If they felt like dancing then they got up and danced. Some of the moves were unusual, but a good time overcame any inhibitions.

The air was warm inside the shed. In search of a cool drink, Kathy pushed through the throng surrounding the bar. While she was waiting her turn, a man alongside her turned abruptly with a clutch of drinks and jostled against her. The shove was just enough to unbalance her on the high-heeled shoes. Kathy lurched to one side, flailing slightly and struggling to regain her balance.

"Watch out!" An angry voice protested as Kathy stumbled against another reveller. Melissa Gilbert was holding the remains of her drink, some of which had spilt down the front of her dress leaving incriminating streaks against the silky fabric.

"Oh, I'm so sorry," Kathy said. "I didn't mean to bump you. Here, perhaps this will dry off the spots." She proffered a paper serviette from the pile that was sitting on the bar.

"Don't rub it in. You'll only make it worse!" Melissa snapped.

Kathy's cheeks flushed with humiliation as Melissa threw one last glare in her direction and pushed through the crowd. The woman must have driven back home to get ready for the ball. Her outfit would have originated in some exclusive boutique in a city, and the careful styling that accompanied it had not been accomplished in a tent.

Feeling nondescript by comparison and curiously flat, Kathy wandered outside and paused in the dark shadows of a tree, listening to the muted sounds of the band. The break provided a welcome contrast to the frivolity inside. She patted her burning cheeks lightly, hoping for cool relief from the night air. Belatedly she realised she hadn't stopped to get a drink, and she was still thirsty. Horrid woman—she hadn't meant to bump her. She felt like being alone for a while.

Approaching footsteps broke into her reverie. Conscious of being out in the dark alone, Kathy turned and saw the outline of a man approaching. Her heart skipped a beat. She was poised to run, except that she couldn't in her strappy shoes.

Alex Woodleigh loomed before her. He had the lights of the hall behind him, and his face was masked in silhouette. She was very much aware of his proximity, and the shielded grey eyes that reflected a glint from the outside lighting. His silhouette was somehow ominous and unsettling. What did he want? Was he going to ask her to pay for cleaning Melissa's dress or something like that? *Oh, give me a break.*

"Out here all alone? Are you sure that's safe for a city girl?" he drawled. "Where are your playmates? Don't they know you need someone to look after you?"

"Shouldn't you be dancing with Melissa?" she retaliated. "I prefer to be alone, thank you."

Kathy felt hemmed in with the tree on one side and Alex on the other. She looked for an opportunity to squeeze past him. There was no way she wanted to remain so close. Where were Chris and Mark when she needed them? Sadly, she knew full well where they were, as she had spied both of them on the dance floor as she headed for the bar. They had spread themselves around the women at the ball, single or not, quite determined to have a good time.

"You're not safe to be on your own in this country." His tone was softly derisive. "You're so out of place. You can't even change a tyre, amongst other things."

"Oh, and Melissa Gilbert can I suppose? As if she's going to damage her finger nails doing battle with a wheel brace. Go back and look after her instead of annoying me." Kathy made no attempt to disguise her hostility, and made to duck around him.

"You'll have to do a whole lot better if you think you'll find a husband in these parts, or is the helpless act part of the strategy?" He moved slightly to the side, blocking her path back to the shed and also obscuring her from the view of anyone else. Kathy looked at him in confusion.

"Perhaps," he said, after a moment's loaded silence, "you have a few more desirable attributes."

The look he gave her was speculative, but unreadable in relation to what was on his mind. Kathy felt a swirl of emotions. There was something magnetic about the man, but this was not the time or place to examine whether that inspired attraction or repulsion. She needed to put some distance between them.

She tried to take a step back but the tree blocked her path. Ignoring her obvious incomprehension, Alex reached out and slid a finger down one side of her face, finishing at the corner of her mouth. His expression mesmerised her, leaving her rooted to the spot and locked to his gaze. He grasped her by the shoulders, pulling her firmly towards him. As her lips opened in protest, she realised she didn't want to. Before she could utter a single word, he lowered his mouth on hers, one hand sliding down to the small of her bare back to press her even closer.

It seemed as if the lights went out, and not only because of the bulk positioned between her and the electric illumination. The strength in the man that she had already observed was apparent, and up close that magnetic field seemed to suck her into his orbit and tight embrace. She could scarcely breathe. His lips claimed hers with an arrogance that left her gasping yet sent electric quivers to her core, seemingly now molten. Her knees would have given way if he weren't holding her so tightly.

The realization that she had responded to his overtures suddenly jerked her back to reality. Her body had betrayed her. With surprising strength, Kathy pushed him away.

"Get away from me." Her anger masked her embarrassment at the wave of heat that surged through her body.

"I might have been mistaken, but you seemed to enjoy being kissed. I thought there might be a degree of passion beneath that prim exterior."

She was mortified. His kiss had stirred startling sensations, but she wasn't going to let him know that. She didn't even understand why she had reacted as she did.

His eyes hovered over her outfit. "Did I say that green suits you very well? Fits nicely in all the right places too."

Kathy looked at him with disgust. "You bastard! Keep your hands to yourself."

Alex laughed. "Say you didn't like it. Try to tell me you didn't respond."

"Kathy? Are you out there? Don't you owe me a dance?"

As Kathy looked towards the shed, she could see a silhouetted figure peering into the darkness. *Thank God! Mark, you're just in time!*

"Well look who's here; one of the boyfriends. At least you've got some early practice in. Have a nice time."

As he turned and walked back into the hall, Kathy wiped her mouth furiously. She paused for a moment, giving Alex time to enter the hall before emerging from the shadows. It would be too awful if anyone had seen that little encounter. Fortunately, Mark wouldn't have been able to see past the exterior lighting.

Walking to meet her unknowing saviour, Kathy resolved not to be alone with Alex Woodleigh again if she could help it. The very thought of him touching her filled her with loathing. He was everything that she detested in a man! If only she could forget the sensation of his lips against hers.

CHAPTER 5

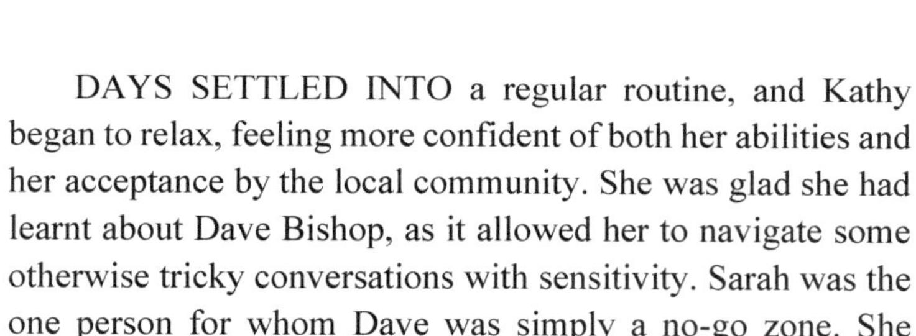

DAYS SETTLED INTO a regular routine, and Kathy began to relax, feeling more confident of both her abilities and her acceptance by the local community. She was glad she had learnt about Dave Bishop, as it allowed her to navigate some otherwise tricky conversations with sensitivity. Sarah was the one person for whom Dave was simply a no-go zone. She made it clear that she didn't want to discuss him or their relationship. At all. This surprised Kathy as it challenged her perception of Sarah's open and forthright personality, but she respected everyone's right to grieve in their own way.

Kathy loved the flying and the novelty of her flying days, but she also looked forward to her rostered days off. She joined the local library and discovered the town swimming pool. Patronage was low mid-week when students were in school, and she could command a lane for long fluid laps, relishing the opportunity to stretch and give her shoulder muscles a workout. It helped to counteract the long hours spent sitting at the controls.

She also put some time into exploring the town and its surrounds, and checking out the coffee shops. She ran into Rose Woodleigh one day in an arcade off the main street.

"Kathy dear, how nice to see you. Not working today?"

Rose carried a shopping bag bearing the name of a local boutique. In contrast to the other casually dressed people who were meandering past or window shopping, Rose was immaculately turned out. Kathy had the feeling that she was not one to ever let standards drop.

"Hi Rose. This is my rostered day off. Looks like you've been catching up with some shopping."

"I like to make the most of my time in town. I was at the hair dresser's first thing this morning and then I thought I could treat myself to a new blouse. I ended up with rather more than that," she added ruefully.

"Your hair looks lovely. You'll have to give me some advice on who is the best stylist in town. Finding a good cutter can be a challenge. Do you have time for a coffee? I'd love you to join me."

The two women settled down to a comfortable chat, fuelled with good coffee and satisfyingly decadent chocolate cake.

"You've such a slim figure Kathy," said Rose as she suggested the treat. "You can afford a little indulgence now and then."

"Rose, you're in pretty fine form yourself. It doesn't look as though you've caved in to rich appetites very often."

"Well, cooking for men on the station, I've had to keep a reasonable supply of baked treats coming out of my kitchen. They have such huge appetites. I've kept myself busy though and don't like to let myself go."

Kathy nodded. She knew all about those appetites, and it wasn't just for food.

"I heard you went to the Hart's Range Races," Rose added. "Did you enjoy it?"

"I did. I had no idea what to expect, but it was quite an experience."

Presumably Alex had told his mother she'd been there. If not him, the local grapevine would have done so—Tom Daly perhaps.

"I saw Alex and Melissa there. They seemed to be enjoying themselves."

"They go every year—have done since they were children. Melissa's been a good friend to Alex, especially when he needed support. That boy of mine has a tough exterior, but events in the last year have caused him to question a lot of things he took for granted."

That was an odd comment, but Kathy didn't query it. She didn't want to seem overly inquisitive. She waited, but nothing further was said on the subject.

When they parted, Rose leaned forward and kissed Kathy on the cheek.

"Thank you for coffee, my dear. It's always nice to sit down and have a chat. Must go. Lots to do when I come to town and I still need to visit an old friend."

She really is a lovely person, Kathy reflected as she watched Rose make her way past the groups of tourists and out of the arcade. Pity it's not a family trait.

"It's good to meet you at last. I've seen you around the airport of course but somehow our paths never directly crossed. Welcome, both to Alice and to the Club."

The Aero Club president engulfed Kathy's hand in his and pumped it up and down after she eventually wandered inside. After weeks of passing the Club rooms, she thought she should investigate her eligibility for membership. She had belonged to a similar Club in Adelaide and found it a supportive environment for anyone involved in aviation. Getting involved in the club would be a good way to meet more people. Often members gathered on weekends and shared a friendly drink after the day's flying—and shared flying stories of course.

"You'll have to come out and show us how it's done," the President continued. "This Sunday is competition day."

He explained that once a month, the club held flying competitions, testing participants for their skills in various flying manoeuvres.

"It's often the newer pilots who have the sharpest skills and so score the highest points, and don't they just love that," he said. "It's a fun event, but also an easy way for members to review their weak points and find out what techniques need revision."

"You can go one better than that."

They were joined by another man almost as wide as he was tall, introduced as Bruce. He'd been listening to the conversation and Kathy had sensed he waited for the right moment to break in. Bruce was introduced as the social coordinator. He planned new events and then had to encourage people to participate. He hitched the band of his trousers up over his obstructive belly. Kathy noticed they just slipped down again, and tried not to keep looking at this as he continued.

"If you really want to have some fun, you need to come along to the weekend fly-in next month. We're heading out to Tom Daly's property at Jinka Station. It'll be a camping trip, so you need to take a swag and some basic creature comforts. Some will drive out, but most will fly, if not in the club's aircraft, then in their own. On the Sunday morning, we'll use the airstrip at Jinka for the competition. The details won't be announced until the day because the instructors organise that, but it's my bet it'll include a flour bombing competition."

"Sounds… fun," she said dryly. "The surrounding country must be coated in splattered flour. Isn't that some sort of environmental hazard?"

"Ah, the ants 'll soon clear up that lot. Whaddyer say? Are you going to come out there with us?"

"Sounds like an offer too good to refuse. It depends on my roster and no promises, but I'll think about it."

"Good on yer Kathy. Stick your name up on the board if you want to share an aircraft with someone. Keeps the costs down that way."

Bruce ambled off, and Kathy did put her name down before introducing herself to other members, most of whom she already knew. She probably would go. It would broaden her local experience and if there was a conflict with her roster, there was still enough time to address that. The other question to resolve, assuming she did go, was what she needed to take with her.

When in doubt, ask Sarah, the fountain of all local knowledge. Kathy brought it up that evening, back at the flats.

"Why don't you come too, Sarah? Lots of people you know will be there."

"There will be, and in part, that's why I don't want to come this time. I went last year— with Dave — and it was the last trip that we were able to make together. It probably sounds emotional but to go back this year on my own would be confronting. I'd rather keep the memories of the time we shared intact."

"Sarah, I should have thought of that. I'm sorry."

"Don't be silly. You couldn't have known and there's nothing to be sorry about." She changed the subject in her usual manner, and Kathy knew enough now to leave it alone. Sarah had only mentioned Dave once before.

"Chris or Mark will have a swag you could borrow, but I have a small two-person tent you can take if you like. I prefer the tent because it gives me more privacy. I also have a small fold-up chair and an air mattress. If you take your sleeping bag, you should be set. Probably a utility will drive to the camp site, taking the bulky gear and cooking supplies, etc. There'll be a limit to how much you can take in the plane. I assume you'll go out in one of the club's four-seaters?"

"That's the intention. I'm flying out with a girl who has just got her licence. She's jumped at the opportunity to fly with another female. She wants to get her hours up." Kathy grinned. "I can sit back for a change and take it easy. I never imagined when I was first qualified that I would take that view. I was eager to get all the flying time that I could."

Arrangements were confirmed over the next couple of weeks, and it was arranged Kathy would act as navigator while Angela did the flying. They were also taking a couple of passengers who were students with the Club. As Sarah had

85

flagged, there wasn't the capacity in the luggage compartment to take more than basic survival requirements, so their camping gear was loaded into the utility which left early on the Saturday morning, with Bruce at the wheel.

He leaned from the window as he reversed from the parking spot behind the club house.

"See ya, ladies. I'll race you there."

"You probably will, Bruce," called Kathy. "Drive carefully."

The flight went according to plan with a smooth landing, much to Angela's expressed relief. She was still self-conscious. Bruce wasn't there, but he rolled in about an hour later and they claimed their belongings from the tray of the utility. Fortunately, the luggage had been covered with a tarp, for the road was dusty as reflected by the red film covering the vehicle.

Retrieving her gear, Kathy looked around for somewhere to pitch her tent. Tom had designated a general camp site area not far from the strip and had collected a pile of firewood for the campers. The site had been used before, and a rough circle of stones indicated the location of past fires. She didn't want to be too far away, but sought some privacy. She carted everything to a smaller clearing, shielded from the main camp by some low-set shrubs and spread out the base of the tent.

"Need some help?"

That sounded like…couldn't be… but there he stood. Alex Woodleigh. *What's he doing here?* She hadn't seen him since the night at the Ball and the memory still rankled. It hadn't occurred to her he might attend this weekend jaunt. She'd assumed mostly town-based pilots would attend a fly-in, not those from the stations. If she'd realised, she might not have come.

"No thank you. I can manage quite well on my own."

"I'm sure you can. I was just asking if you would like some help. It's quicker with some assistance and…"

"Don't say it! … and city girls probably don't know how to put up a tent anyway. This one does so thank you for the offer but I'm fine."

"Well, I wouldn't put it there if I were you. Not unless you want to have ants in your pants."

Only then did Kathy see the ant's nest adjacent to the spot she had chosen, with the ant trail running right under the floor of the tent. *Damn. What a stupid mistake to make.* Now she did feel like a novice.

"Up to you entirely of course," Alex continued in an irritating drawl, "but I suggest looking over here. There are no ants, which is a good start; the site is level, which is another plus; there are no big gum trees to drop branches on you in the middle of the night; and lastly, it's far enough away from the camp fire that you should be able to go to sleep if the die-hards carry on tonight."

Kathy hated to admit it, but he was right. She couldn't see a better location. After gathering up the tent, she stumbled towards the new spot, trying to see above the armful of slippery nylon and to avoid tripping on the guy ropes now dragging along the ground and snagging in the odd prickle bush.

"You spread it out where you want," Alex said, "and I'll get the mallet from the back of the ute. I assume you don't already have it?"

Kathy's flush increased. She had forgotten about the mallet. "Um, thanks," she muttered. "I was going to get it after I was more organised."

He strode off, leaving Kathy to separate the tent from the fly and to position it how she wanted. *I would have thought about the mallet soon enough. It's not as though I was going to bash the pegs in with rocks.*

And then he was back, doing the bloke thing and keeping control of the mallet and driving the pegs into the ground with steady, well-directed blows. She wished he'd just go away, even though it would be easier and quicker with two pairs of hands. It only left her to blow up the air bed and to put her gear inside the tent.

"That's about it. I'll take the mallet back. Someone else might need it." As he spoke, Alex brushed the dirt off his hands on the back of his jeans, drawing her eyes momentarily to his compact derriere. Her mind wandered to possibilities, quickly repressed. She only gave his butt a quick glance, but the tug at the corner of his mouth made her think that he'd probably caught the look. *What was it with him always watching her?*

"Thank you," she said stiffly.

"Any time," he said, with a slight incline of his head. "Always pleased to be of service to a lady."

He turned back towards the main camp, absolving her from the need to respond further. She watched that tight muscular derriere again. Unless Alex had eyes in the back of his head, he wouldn't see her this time. She smiled inwardly before going to check on Angela in case she needed any assistance in setting up her camp site.

People were still trickling in, some flying and others driving. There were no flying activities planned for the day, so the focus was more on establishing the camp, socialising and of course refreshments, mostly of the liquid type. Camp operations were overseen by Tom Daly, who had an opinion on most things and was generous in his willingness to share them. He was a well-known and well-loved local character though, and people respected his local knowledge, acquired over many decades.

"And how are you young Kathy?" Tom enquired. "About time you came out to my place. Haven't got yerself lost yet?"

"I'm well thank you Tom, and all the better for seeing you. No, I haven't got myself lost at all. It's been a steep learning curve since I arrived but I'm reasonably familiar with much of the country now."

"I'm pleased to hear it. Not good country to be lost in. I grew up here so I know it like the back of my hand. Spent a lot of time with the local Aborigines when I was a lad too, so I learnt a lot from the old blokes. Not many of them left now though."

He sniffed reflectively. It occurred to Kathy that if the old blokes were 'old' when Tom was a lad, they were hardly likely to still be around. She refrained from expressing the view, being sure that although Tom might concede that he was getting on in years, he would not own up to being old.

Not as tall as he probably once was, he had the textured skin that reflected a lifetime in a harsh environment. His hair was snowy white, but rarely seen beyond wispy bits, as he wasn't known to take his hat off. His eyes were a little watery, but they didn't miss much and what he didn't see, the bush telegraph soon told him.

"I'll have look around Jinka while I have the opportunity. Are you on your own out here?"

"Sort of, Kathy. My nephews run the place now and Alex Woodleigh comes over occasionally to help out with bore runs. I get some help when it's branding or mustering time, but I still do a few things m'self. Wasn't always like that, but there you go. Mary's in town and I'm out here. Times change.

"Mary? I don't think I've met Mary. Is she your…?"

"My wife — yes Mary's my wife. She's got that Parkinson's Disease. I kept her here as long as I could but it became difficult. I could be gone for hours, couple of days sometimes if I was working on a far part of the property and Mary needed more care than I could give her. We're so far from help. It was a difficult decision but I think she was relieved in the end."

He avoided direct eye-contact, gazing instead into the distance. Kathy's heart ached for him, and the sadness he must surely be feeling. There was a pause before he continued.

"She's got more company in town, and the staff from the nursing home are very good with her. I get into town when I can and her old friends visit as well. Nothing wrong with her mind; it's just her body that's gone to pieces."

"Tom, you must miss her dreadfully. Did you have any children?"

"Yeah, two. A girl and a boy." His voice took on a flatter tone. "Elizabeth went to school in the city and never came back. There were visits of course, but after school there was university and then she met some city bloke and now they and the kids lead a city life. Don't see them much. It's a long way to come, isn't it, and I don't go down there very often. There's nothing to do in the city so I just turn around and come home again."

"I'm sure they love seeing you though," soothed Kathy, not sure what else to say. "What about your son? Did he end up moving away as well?"

"In a way, but more permanently, so to speak. There was an accident some twenty years ago now. Richard was out checking the bores on the motor bike and came off. Something must have spooked him or got in the way because he was a good rider. We didn't miss him immediately, and then it took a while before we found him. We called in the air ambulance but his injuries were pretty bad and he didn't make it."

"Tom, I can't believe what dreadful bad luck you've had." She wished now she hadn't asked about his son.

"Yeah, well — that's life, isn't it?" He swiped dismissively at an irritating fly that was buzzing under the brim of his hat. "You just have to pick yourself up and move on."

"Yes, I know, but still…" She trailed off. "What nursing home is Mary in now? I assume it's in Alice? I could visit her sometimes if you like. I'll take her some photos of this weekend. I'm sure she would like an update on what's happening."

"That'd be real nice of you Kathy. She always loves a visit and she's heard about you. I keep her up to date on all the news when I get into town. I told her there was this new young sheila flying around in Dave Bishop's place."

Kathy winced. "Nothing stays secret around here for very long, does it? Does she read much? I could take her some magazines as well."

"Reading's not so easy for her now, but she has one of them cassette player things. Sometimes she gets talking books from the library and of course she can listen to the radio as well."

"Look, I'll visit her and have a chat first. Then I can see what she would like and take it from there." Impulsively, she reached out and gave the old man a hug. "I'm sorry you and your family have had such a raw deal Tom. I think it's fantastic the way you've coped out here on your own."

Tom, clearly not used to such close physical contact, especially with a young woman, blushed a tanned shade of puce before returning the hug, gingerly at first and then with more emotion before extricating himself.

"Look here, people will start talking if they see me cavorting with an attractive young sheila like you. I'd better see how the camp fire is going."

He ambled off, adjusting his hat back to its original position as he went. On turning to go back to her tent, Kathy realised that Alex Woodleigh was standing a short distance away, and had observed her interaction with Tom. He was stony-faced.

"Visiting Mary would be a good idea—she's a good woman who has been dealt a raw deal. Just don't go making any promises you can't or don't intend to keep. She's not a passing diversion just so you can feel good about yourself."

How long have you been listening in? "Sure, I'm just going to entertain myself for a while before disappearing back to Adelaide. What else would a young city-slicker do?" She kept her voice low, not wanting others to hear, but not disguising her hostility.

"Must you always grab the wrong end of the stick? I was just saying, that's all. I've known Tom and Mary a long time and would hate to see them messed around, particularly Mary."

He didn't wait for a reply, but turned and headed for one of the fireside groups, where he joined the conversation without a backwards glance. *I don't know anyone who can get under my skin as much as that man.* Kathy swiped at some bush flies with impatience. She would keep out of his way over the weekend. If she stuck with other people, it would minimise any interaction they might otherwise have.

Keeping to this decision, she went for a bush walk with Angela and their two passengers. Tom had told them about a gorge that was about a kilometre away. She wanted some exercise and the gorge sounded attractive. She took her camera, intent on getting photos for Mary as well as some for her own benefit.

The exercise associated with the walk felt good after sitting in the aircraft, and there was plenty to look at along the way. A creek ran through the gorge, leading from a rock pool at the far end. To her surprise, Kathy could hear the croak of frogs and judging by the footprints at the water's edge, various birds and animals also came along for a drink. Sitting on a poolside rock and dabbling her feet in the icy water, she reflected on the weekend thus far. The person she least wanted to see was Alex Woodleigh. Why was it then that she couldn't get him out of her thoughts?

***

It took her a while to work out where she was. Piccaninny dawn crept across the sky, but not much light showed in the tent. She lay there, listening to the dawn chorus, trying to identify the calls she could hear. She felt warm snuggled up in her sleeping bag, but the tip of her nose told her that the temperature was chilly outside of the covers. That was a pity, as she had a pressing need to relieve her bladder. She peeled herself out of the downy cocoon inside the tent, and wriggled into her jeans whilst still lying on her back. She slipped on her boots after shaking them carefully to ensure that no nocturnal visitors lurked in the toes.

The camp was still, though not entirely quiet, as sounds of snoring could clearly be heard from another tent. Kathy eased the zip closure up slowly, anxious not to rent the morning air with the metallic rip. She straightened up gingerly, her knees creaking a protest. With hands on hips, she arched back, stretching the kinks from her spine. Looking around, she couldn't see any activity from the neighbouring tents. No one had been disturbed.

There were no designated latrine facilities, so a tree wee was the order of the day. There was a drum of water, a bowl, and roll of toilet paper and a hand trowel, making up the accoutrements of the bush bathroom. Taking the trowel and roll of paper, she made her way up the hill behind the camp site, seeking the shelter of the bushes. She knew no one else was about, but modesty still dictated some privacy. Climbing to a fair height, she checked back to consider visibility. All good. She couldn't see the campsite and so deduced the campsite wouldn't see her as she went about her business. She couldn't wait any longer.

She had a lovely view out over the plains, and was delighted when she saw a mob of kangaroos, gently undulating down the slope. The light had increased enough to allow her to pick them out from the dull greens, browns and ochres of the surrounding scrub when they rose above the vegetation. This time of day was special. She completed her task and walked a few steps away to better admire the view.

"You're up early."

What? Kathy spun around. *Surely Alex Woodleigh hadn't been watching while she…* She flushed at the thought, feeling the heat in the tips of her ears in contrast to the chilling morning.

"How long have you been there? Were you watching me?"

"I never watch a lady going about her private business."

She looked down at the roll of toilet paper she carried. It was a dead giveaway as to her primary purpose for climbing the hill. She shouldn't have felt embarrassed, but she did.

"I was already here when you crawled out of your tent and headed up in this direction," he said. "Don't worry. The bushes provided a good screen. Your modesty was protected."

"Couldn't you have coughed or something?"

"You were a woman on a mission and I didn't want to alarm you in the half light."

Kathy stared at him, suspicion still in her eyes. Her heart raced in response to her initial fright.

"I didn't think anyone else was up."

"Waking early is a habit, one that's hard to break. Once I'm awake, I feel I might as well get up. I came up here for a similar reason, and of course to salute the dawn."

He looked at her with a hint of a smile. She looked twice to confirm she hadn't imagined it. She must have still looked perturbed, for he made the effort to reassure her.

"You followed me shortly after and to repeat, yes you were well screened."

"Pleased about that." She couldn't think of anything else to say. *Do you come here often?* didn't seem appropriate. She turned to go.

"I guess I'll get back down to the camp."

"Why? Nobody else is up yet. What will you do?"

"Uh—go for a walk, I guess."

"A city girl like you might get herself lost out here, or fall down a rabbit hole just like Alice." He paused. "It's like Wonderland, isn't it? There's probably even the odd mad hatter around, although the cats are feral, not Cheshire."

Kathy looked at him askance. This conversation was not what she'd expected when she had crawled out of her tent. Just when she thought she had this man summed up, he turned around and surprised her.

"Come on," he said. "If you want to go for a walk, we might as well go together."

"But…" Kathy gestured with the roll of toilet paper and the trowel which she still held, feeling faintly ridiculous. "I should take it back to the camp. Someone might need it."

He snorted. "They'll cope. I shouldn't imagine that the blokes will have too much trouble. Leave it here and we'll pick it up on the way back."

Glancing once more at the camp site to reassure herself no one else was stirring, Kathy did as he suggested.

Alex led the way across the apex of the hill, picking a path between the spinifex grass and rocky outcrops, clearly expecting she would fall in behind. The assumption annoyed her, but she found following in his footsteps easier than finding her own path through the spikey plants.

The muted light edged across the sky, bathing the landscape in soft pastel colours. With the camp no longer in view, it seemed they were the only two people in an alien yet beautiful landscape.

Not quite alone. Alex pointed out a dingo some fifty metres away, slinking close to the ground. A skinny buff-coloured animal, it blended with the landscape as it moved purposefully through the scrub.

Kathy was intrigued when Alex indicated the dog. She might not have noticed it if she'd been on her own.

There were other things he showed her as well. The bearded dragon was difficult to see against the mottled rocks, particularly as it froze on their approach. Alex picked it up, and while Kathy was fascinated with her close-up inspection, she was not in any hurry to handle the reptile herself. When he put it down, it scurried away, putting distance between itself and the intruders.

She had some sympathy for the reptile as she was equally disconcerted with her proximity to her companion. She couldn't scurry away as easily. The experience was very different to the previous time she was this close to the man. Just thinking of that occasion raised some challenging memories.

He also showed her various bush plants, explaining which were a source of food for the local Aborigines.

"You see this one?" he said. "If you take a digging stick and poke around the roots, you might be lucky enough to find some of the grubs that habitually live there. Good source of tasty protein."

"Euww—I'll stick to eggs and bacon."

"That's fine if you can get it. Of course, you might find some goanna eggs but I wouldn't expect any at this time of year. You need to find the goanna tracks first before you can find the eggs. On the other hand, you can eat the berries from this bush. Here—try one.”

The berry was small and very sour. “Ugh!” Kathy pulled an involuntary grimace. “It’s edible but probably like eating a green lemon.”

“Yeah, well—you have to get your Vitamin C somewhere when you live in the bush.”

“What’s wrong with a Vitamin C tablet? That would be a lot easier to digest than one of those little berries.”

“Sure, that’s a good idea. Why don’t they just pop into the local health food shop?”

“I was only joking. I’m sure it was a valuable food and nutrient source. How come you know this stuff anyway?”

“You know how to survive in the city and I know how to survive out here, including what I might expect to find. I learnt a lot from the local people. A mate and I spent some time with them while growing up.”

“Hmmm—useful information if you’re lost in the bush or living out here like the indigenous people or early settlers were. I’d be really interested in knowing more.”

Alex looked at her speculatively. The look sent a strange ripple down her spine. She was aware of their close proximity. *What was going through his mind?*

“If you stick around long enough, you might learn some more. Not so much if you stay in town all the time though.”

“Mostly I’ll be sitting in a plane. We should probably be getting back to the camp. It’s light now and it’s feeling like time for breakfast. Bacon and eggs with toast on the side I think.” She screwed up her nose. “I’ll leave the witchetty grubs to you. I hope someone’s got the billy on.”

They completed the walk back in companionable silence. When they clambered down a rocky interface, Alex offered Kathy his hand to steady her descent. It seemed entirely natural to take it. She gave him a quick smile of thanks and was rewarded with a brief nod of acknowledgement and a direct look from those grey eyes. They were illuminated by the fresh morning light, and at that close proximity, Kathy realised they weren't completely grey, but flecked with green-gold tints. She had enjoyed the companionship and was bemused in general at the civil tone of the interaction. She hadn't expected that from him. Was this the same man she encountered outside the dance hall at the Harts Range races?

They detoured via their original meeting spot and picked up the items that Kathy had carefully stashed. They were met with some welcoming cries on their return, with Bruce remarking that it was just as well that more than one roll of toilet paper had been bought. Otherwise, things might have been grim.

With breakfast over and the camp cleaned up, the club members gathered for the briefing on the proposed flying competition. As forecast, it did include a flour bombing run, but with a few other technical requirements as well on the circuits that the pilot would make. It sounded quite simple really but from the conversations she had heard, Kathy expected that it wouldn't be.

And it wasn't. There were white splatters covering the ground for some distance fore and aft of the target. She scored her personal best on the final of three bombing runs but conceded she needed a lot more practice. So did the young guns. The old hands crowed with delight as they jockeyed between each other for the winner's trophy.

After the leisurely lunch, punctuated by good-natured bragging on the part of some, campers began packing up and getting ready for the trip home. Those who were flying back to Alice didn't want to be flying into the sun late in the day. Those who were driving didn't want to leave too late and risk the possibility of hitting roos or livestock in the dark. Kathy had already deflated her air mattress and packed up the tent and transferred the heavy items to the back of Bruce's utility.

She caught up with Angela and made sure her flight plan was in order and ready to file. They inspected the aircraft, and checked the fuel for any water contamination. That just left getting everyone boarded and strapped in.

Other pilots and crew made their way to the parking area as well, and there was some jostling to get away quickly and not get stuck behind the queue for take-off. The parking area was midway down the strip, and the aircraft needed to backtrack to gain enough distance for take-off.

Angela paused before moving onto the airstrip. She expressed concern at the number of aircraft queued line up behind her, but was thorough about doing the pre-take off checks and then she taxied right down to the far end of the available strip. She travelled longer than needed to safely take off, but she erred on the side of caution. As Kathy reminded her, she was the pilot in command and so she made the relevant decisions.

As they reached the end of the runway and were about to turn around and line up for take-off, a voice broke in over the radio. Kathy had no difficulty in recognising it.

"Ladies, you're taking forever. Are you thinking of taxiing all the way to Alice or are you lost already? Some of us need to get home. Hold your position while I slip in front of you."

The caller didn't wait for a response. Looking back along the strip, they saw Alex Woodleigh taxi out from the parking area and line up some distance in front of them. He was the only passenger on board his aircraft and so with less weight could depart with a shorter take-off distance. They heard him apply full throttle and next minute his aircraft leapt from the deck and settled into a steady climb.

"Who was *that*?" queried Angela.

"The most arrogant person in Central Australia, that's who. The man's an idiot, pulling a stunt like that. Sadly, you're going to get lots of comments in that vein but don't let them get to you." Privately she was fuming. She had softened her initial view of the man, but now he displayed his true colours. *Just as well he has all that bush knowledge, because that's where he belongs... in the bush.*

CHAPTER 6

THE THICK HEAT oppressed like a heavy blanket. The air shimmered on the horizon; with each breath chokingly hot and thick. Kathy's hair, piled on top of her head, escaped in clammy tendrils. The dampness of her clothes which clung to her did little to give her any relief. Hot and sweaty more like it. Rivulets of moisture trickled between her breasts. The thought of a cold shower kept her going.

She was pleased to be heading back to the office after the morning's charter flight. *Thank God there's no more flights today. I can update flight procedure manuals in the cool of the air-conditioning instead.*

"Ah, Kathy – you're back! Grab a drink and come and look at these charts. You've got some fires to fight." Brian spread out the charts on the table in the hangar office reserved for that purpose.

"Fires? I've no experience with fires." Kathy's heart sank. Standing under the air-conditioning vent, she relished the stream of cool air that was directed down her back. The idea of getting back in that baking aircraft cabin was not one she welcomed.

"Fire spotting," Brian explained. "That's what you'll have to do. After this scorching summer the whole country's a potential fire ball. Outbreaks crop up everywhere when you get embers carried by the wind. There's a big burn happening to the east of Alice and it's a case of all hands on deck. We've got some water bombers on their way from down south but in the meantime, you can direct ground crews to any outbreaks and keep an eye out for anyone who might be in strife."

Brian indicated the areas known to be under threat. "You'll need to go to Arapunya. The Bushfire Council has set up a command centre there and the Divisional Commander will allocate a spotter to go with you."

He looked at her intently. "No risks, Kathy. Keep out of the smoke and maintain visibility at all times. Keep in mind the turbulence you'll get from hot air currents. It may be scorching out there, but this is a day for a cool head."

Hastily eating her lunch as she topped up her water bottle and a spare for good measure, Kathy splashed cold water on her face and freshened up a little before climbing back in the aircraft and setting course for Arapunya with a mixture of excitement and dismay. The concept of a fire so extensive that it could span across miles was awe-inspiring. Bush fire spotting was a challenge she would never have been handed in the city.

Hazy smoke drifted across the horizon. She could smell it. The thought of undertaking a task for which she had no prior experience concerned her, but as Brian had said, she'd have a spotter with her so she wouldn't be alone.

Circling the strip and entering her landing sequence, she spied a cluster of vehicles near the outbuildings to the side of the homestead. While she was still on her final approach, one vehicle detached itself from the others and headed towards the strip to meet her.

"G'day." The driver's grin gave lie to the discomfort of the day. "It's not far, but it seemed mean to make you walk over on a day like today. I'm Mike. Hop in."

Perching on the edge of her seat, which threatened to sear her bottom through the fabric of her trousers, Kathy clutched the dusty dashboard in front of her as the utility bumped and swayed over the dirt track. The command centre had been set up in the station school room, no longer used for that purpose. With a major bush fire, volunteers came from all over. People from neighbouring stations and communities had gathered to offer their help and services. So intent were those in the room on listening to the latest radio report that nobody acknowledged her initially. Straightening up as the report ended, the Commander spotted her and shook her hand in welcome.

"Good to see you. We're not sure what's happening out to the east. We haven't been able to raise Karinya Gorge Homestead on the radio and want to check on that area generally. If you can head off in that direction it would be really helpful.

He showed Kathy the local maps and indicated the grid pattern that he wanted her to fly and where her reporting points should be.

"You shouldn't need to put down, but there are some bush strips in that area. Here, and here." He indicated the locations on the map. "They aren't marked anywhere but whoever goes with you will know where they are. Mike, can you go with Kathy?"

"Sure thing. We'll make a great team. Ready to roll?"

They gathered up the notes and paperwork and headed for the door. He would be an easy travelling companion, reflected Kathy and as a local his familiarity with the country would be reassuring.

"Hey Mike!" A man wearing the firefighting uniform followed them outside. "Have you got a minute? The truck's running rough and I'd like it checked before we take it out again."

"Sorry," he said, turning back to Kathy. "I shouldn't be long. Can you wait a while?"

"It's fine by me but it's up to the Commander. What does he say?"

The Commander didn't have to say much. The frown said it all.

"Look, that wind is picking up out there and I don't like it. I don't like it at all. Best if someone else goes with you and you get going as soon as you can."

His eyes scanned the people remaining in the room. "Alex—what about you? You could do the run with Kathy."

Her heart sank. That man kept turning up like Banquo's ghost. With her attention focused on the Commander, she hadn't realised Alex was in the room.

"Sure," he drawled. "She might get lost on her own."

"I doubt that mate." The Commander was brusque. "I'll fill you in on the grid, then you'd better be on your way."

Alex clearly understood this was not the time for banter and listened carefully. "No worries—you'll hear from us soon, hopefully with the all clear."

Kathy didn't wait but spun on her heels and headed out into a heat so intense that it made her gasp. Another volunteer drove them back to the strip, and she completed some basic pre-flight checks, removed the chocks and clambered aboard, leaving Alex to do the same. Climbing into the passenger's seat seemed to involve almost folding himself in two. It made her appreciate how tall he was. That was about all she appreciated, and beyond a call of 'Clear prop!' directed out the side window, she maintained a frosty silence.

The airstrip was short and Kathy knew she would need the full length on such a hot day. She taxied out from the parking area and back-tracked to the very beginning of the strip, checking the wind sock for wind strength and direction. Once there, she swung the aircraft around in the right direction, and lined up on the centre. Lowering the flaps, she initially stood on the brakes and increased the power on the throttle, watching the needle climb on the tachometer. She had to apply maximum power as quickly if she was going to get off the ground.

Releasing the brakes, they hurtled down the strip and Kathy winced as fine gravel flicked up and flailed against the fuselage. Brian would slaughter her if she chipped the paintwork. The end of the strip was approaching and Kathy pulled back on the control column. The plane eased off the ground and seemed to hover for a while. She lowered the nose slightly and was reassured when the aircraft picked up speed and then settled back into a slow but steady climb. She could relax. Her jaw ached and she realised she had been clenching her teeth.

"Well, at least we're off the ground," the voice beside her drawled. "If you track a course of 021, that will take us to the first check point."

"I know where we have to go. Why don't you look for fires and let me do the flying?"

"Don't get uppity with me. Visibility's not so good, and I know this country like the back of my hand. It will be much easier for both of us if you just accept I might have more local knowledge than you."

Kathy chewed her lip but didn't respond. She didn't want to admit he was right. She prided herself on the precision of her flying, but knew having someone on board who was familiar with the area was practical, even if it had to be Alex Woodleigh.

She thought she heard him mutter "Bloody city women!" but when she glanced at him, he stared out the window on his side.

The air shimmered with haze, but the ground was all clear at the first check point. Kathy had dialled up the radio frequency for the bushfire communications shortly before take-off and she reported back to the Commander before proceeding to the next point on their grid. They over-flew Karinya Gorge and were relieved to see the fires were not close. The homestead was named for the gorge in the range of hills behind it. From the air, the cleft was clearly visible, its progress marked by a creek bed and tall trees, striving to get their share of the sun.

Alex took charge of the radio and tuned to the frequency on which he thought the station might be listening.

"Karinya, this is Mike Yankee Charlie—do you read? Harry, are you there? Give us a call, mate!"

The radio crackled and they could just make out a response.

"Roger, Mike Yankee Charlie. That you Alex? Are you dropping in for a coldie or what?"

"Keep it on ice for me this time Mate. Just checking you're okay… command centre at Arapunya couldn't raise you on the radio or the blower either. From what we can see up here, the nearest fire is about twenty clicks away. The road out of your place looks clear. Keep an eye on that wind. If we see any changes, we'll let you know."

"Roger to that. Thanks Alex. Pass the word along that we're okay and I'll try to reach them also. Over and out.

"Mike Yankee Charlie," Alex acknowledged and slipped the microphone back in its cradle. He gave Kathy the track for the next leg to fly and this time she didn't argue.

They settled into a pattern of work; direction and response, observance and report. There were some fire outbreaks, and they were able to identify the coordinates and report on the location and size, approximating also the wind direction and speed. From the air, Kathy could see the extent of the affected landscape. She hadn't appreciated before just how far or fast the fires could travel. She didn't admit that. It would just invoke another derisive comment.

Alex directed her to bores and along fence lines, checking that equipment was safe, and that cattle were in no danger. Occasionally he asked her to descend to a lower level or to orbit while he got a clearer view of the ground and the infrastructure, but beyond that there was little conversation. The engine noise was not conducive to idle chat.

If the day had seemed hot before, the heat now oppressed. The cabin fans made no difference beyond stirring up the air.

They were closer to the fire, and the flames were visible at a distance. The rising heat created turbulence, which, combined with the temperature of the day meant the flight was bumpy. Holding the aircraft steady and on track was increasingly difficult. Flying required a lot more concentration, meaning the spotting and microphone duties fell to Alex alone.

"Bloody hell!"

Kathy looked around in surprise. Alex peered directly down at the ground from his side window. Dipping the wing slightly so she could see what had taken his attention, she saw a small herd of cattle, trapped by the encroaching fire and huddled up against the fence. The gate in the corner of the paddock was securely shut. There was nothing they could do. Their fate horrified Kathy. It didn't bear thinking about. Surely theirs would be a terrible death.

"Aren't there any other gates or another way out for them? Perhaps they'll jump the fence if the fire gets close."

The glance that Alex cast in her direction was scornful, as was his tone. "The purpose of the fence is to contain the cattle and it's built to a height that they can't jump over. They aren't show ponies, so no—they won't be able to jump over the fence!"

"But there must be something we can do?" She couldn't believe that he was just going to accept their fate as inevitable.

"Yeah? Like what?"

Kathy was too busy scanning the ground below to bother responding. Orbiting to get a clearer view of the area, she could just make out a track that ran parallel to and some five metres from the fence. The dirt surface was rutted in places, but from their height she couldn't see any rocks or significant obstructions. There was a substantial section that was relatively straight, and with low grassy vegetation on either side. If she made a very careful approach, she could touch down and pull up close to the fence. Provided the wind didn't increase and there weren't any major pot holes she couldn't see from the air, there would be time to let the cattle out, taxi back along the track, and take off again.

The plume of smoke gave her an indication of wind direction and she was satisfied she could land into wind. She changed heading to manoeuvre the aircraft into the landing sequence.

"Fasten your seat belt—we may be in for a rough landing!"

"What are doing? Are you crazy? You can't put down there! We'll burn alive, woman. You've no idea how fast those flames can travel."

Alex's voice was strained. He sounded horrified, and not without good reason. Kathy's stomach churned, but she wasn't going to let him know. *At least, given that I am already dripping with sweat, I don't have to pretend to be cool, calm and collected.* Trimming the aircraft for descent, Kathy pointed out the track and explained her plan. Alex's frown deepened.

"You need your head read, contemplating a kamikaze stunt like that! I wish there was something that we could do for the cattle but there's nothing to be gained by stacking the plane and burning ourselves to a crisp. You can't do it."

"Shut up and get ready. Jump out and open the gate while I turn the plane. If you don't want to, then you can just sit here and wait while I open the gate instead."

Alex raised both hands in resigned supplication. Kathy briefly took her eyes off the landing point ahead and took in the grimness of his look. She was vaguely aware of his pre-landing preparations. He checked the tightness of his belt and stowed all loose articles then unlocked the passenger door and opened it just a fraction. The slipstream held it in a closed position. In the event that she stacked the plane, it would be easier to evacuate the wreckage if the door wasn't locked or jammed. His final action was to brace himself against the dashboard as landing approached.

Kathy touched down with a thump. Not one of her better landings; more of a drop onto the ground. Taxiing faster than was strictly safe, she covered the distance to the gate and jammed on the brakes, skidding slightly in the loose dust. Alex leapt out and sprinted for the gate as the cattle, startled by this intrusion, scattered a short distance away, bellowing their distress.

The gate was held secure with a heavy length of chain, with the ring at the end slipped over a bolt. He seemed to fiddle with it forever, but finally the chain was free and he dragged the gate open, propping a large stone against it to hold it in that position. He ran, whooping at the cattle, activating a mini stampede towards safety. That accomplished, he turned and sprinted for the plane. Kathy had swung the plane around, ready to move off and watched his progress anxiously. She wasn't confident they would make it out of there.

Alex was still shutting the door and scrabbling for his seat belt when she pushed the throttle forward and taxied at speed back down the track, far enough to turn around for a take-off into wind. Tendrils of smoke swirled in front of them. Any more and her vision would be obscured. She was already blinking with the irritation. Her hands were clammy on the control column. She was scared; really scared.

"Go girl, go!"

Kathy didn't need telling. She was so frightened she felt sick to her stomach. She lowered a stage of flap and yanked back on the controls, forcing the plane into the air.

"Do you realize you almost collected the fence at the end of the paddock?" Alex sounded incredulous. "You might want to save the aerobatics for when you are on your own." He paused a moment. "Still, good flying, all things considered."

Turning to look at him, Kathy was astonished to find that he was grinning at her. Not a sense of humour, surely! Overwhelmed with relief at the job accomplished and a sense of absurdity, she threw back her head and laughed. The tremor in her knees as she held the rudder steady made her aware of the tension coursing through her body. *That was one helluva landing— and take-off for that matter*. She shook her head as the realisation of what she had just done hit her. She caught Alex looking at her with a similar expression. Their eyes met and quickly Kathy looked away, feeling inexplicably quite vulnerable.

The tension between them was dissolving. She was aware of it. She was also very much aware of the heat.

The next direction Alex gave surprised Kathy. It wasn't part of their schedule and nowhere near the fires. When she queried him, he answered enigmatically that he'd had enough of heat and smoke for the time being. That was understandable but surely they should be sticking to their designated grid? Challenging him would threaten the current mood. All she got from him was a half smirk before he turned to peer out the window, clearly looking for landmarks.

At his direction, she found herself over a bush strip which had been made alongside a local bore. It sat beside the banks of the Elkedra River, the surprising waterway which Brian had shown her on their first flight together. She landed and pulled up in the shade of a gnarled and twisted tree on the edge of the strip. This landing was a piece of cake in comparison to her previous effort.

"What are we doing here? I can't see any more cattle."

Alex had already opened his door and was clambering out. Only as he looked back at her did she see the sooty smudge on his face.

"Hurry up. It's time to cool off. I need it, even if you don't."

Climbing out, she secured the aircraft and hurried after him, still puzzled.

A bend in the river was shaded by local trees. The banks were steep and sliding down the edge towards the water, Kathy felt as though she was entering a small microcosm. The air was cooler and insects hovered above the surface of the water. The pool nestling in the bend was an unexpected delight. She made her way down the bank, marvelling at the unexpected vista. Alex watched her reaction.

"It's a favourite haunt," he explained. "I've been coming here for years. It never dries up—not even in summer. Not many people know about it. Just the locals and of course the first inhabitants. It had special significance to them. You can understand why."

The water looked so inviting. At least she could have a paddle and cool off if it wasn't too deep at the edges. Kathy turned to ask Alex and blushed a brilliant crimson when she saw he had already taken off his shirt, and was in the process of removing his jeans.

"What are you doing?"

"I would have thought that was obvious. You can do what you like, but I'm going for a dip."

Clad only in his jocks, he strode over to the edge of the bank and executed a perfect dive into the water. Surfacing, he swam with sure steady strokes towards the centre.

Even through the water, Kathy could see the fine muscle tone of his body. Realising he had stopped and was looking at her, she flushed and looked away. The heat must be getting to her or something.

"What are you waiting for? It's beautiful in." He trod water and watched her, a bemused expression in his face. "Don't tell me you can't swim. I had the impression that you could do anything!"

Her chin lifted a fraction. Without further contemplation, Kathy slipped out of her outer clothes, and paused hesitantly on the edge of the bank, clad in lace panties and matching bra. Just like a bikini really, she told herself, and stepped gingerly into the water before sliding beneath the surface.

The cold water made her gasp, but the sensation felt exhilarating. Kathy couldn't remember when she'd last had fun like this. She'd missed that. Life had been serious as of late. It felt good to let her hair down.

As a swimmer, Kathy was every match for Alex. With all thoughts of the fires far behind them, they swam and frolicked like a pair of kids. She swam to the far side of the pool and then flipped onto her back and floated for a while, protected by the dappled shade from the adjacent trees. She drifted into a blissful state, until Alex duck-dived under water and grabbed one of her ankles, dragging her down. She shrieked and pushed him back under when he surfaced. Finally exhausted, they pulled themselves out of the water.

"If I had a towel, I would offer you one, but on second thoughts, I think I like you better without." Looking down, Kathy could see that her flimsy underwear had become almost transparent with its soaking, and its effect was clearly not lost on Alex. She was mortified. She made every effort not to look at him, but found his proximity disturbing. She felt both vulnerable and exposed.

My clothes! Too bad if I'm wet— I've got to get my clothes on.

"Looking for something?" The drawl was teasingly soft.

Looking up, Kathy saw that Alex was holding her blouse and trousers. How was it she hadn't seen him pick them up? She reached out to grab them. He snagged her wrist with his hand, drawing her closer to him. This wasn't the time for games! Her protest, was stifled by the look that was in his eyes. Her breath quickened, and she was overwhelmed by an indefinable feeling, conscious only of the pressure of his thighs against hers.

All further thoughts were lost in a wave of sensation as he lowered his lips to hers, claiming a gentle and caressing kiss. She resisted briefly, and then surrendered to the warm sweet waves that engulfed her. She had kissed men before, but this was different. She was confused by the emotions that swirled through her body. There was the undeniable feeling of wanting more. The sensation was unreal. Kathy placed her hands on his chest and pushed slightly away so she could look up at him. Confused thoughts streamed through her head.

"This is crazy," she whispered. "We don't even like each other!"

"There's a lot of what you do and say that gets under my skin, and that's part of the problem. There are few women who stir me up like you do. I sure like what you do to me. I especially like what you're doing to me now."

"And what… am I…doing to you?" she whispered, as she wound one hand behind his neck and ran the other over his chest, pressing herself even closer, if that was possible.

"Sending me crazy, as if you didn't know. Do you want to stop?"

"No. No I don't. Maybe I'm a little crazy too."

He moaned softly in response, claiming her lips again, nibbling softly at the corners before kissing her more deeply. Kathy felt she should still make some level of protest.

"But the fires—we're helping with the fires!"

"Believe me, you're helping this fire." Desire was evident in his eyes as he drew her closer again.

"We shouldn't be here. I don't usually..."

"I'm glad. Stop talking and kiss me again."

Maintaining eye contact, which was a sensual act in itself, his fingers moved with a life of their own, sensing, probing and then gently caressing. Kathy no longer objected as he deftly unhooked the catch of her bra, and eased the filmy lace from her breasts, releasing them to the tantalising caress of the breeze, his hands, and finally his tongue. Her nipples swelled in response. She wanted him to touch her. *More, harder, don't stop!* He stirred feelings of such delicious urgency.

He eased her back onto the soft grass on the river bank, and planted soft fairy kisses across her stomach, gently removing her panties and the last of her modesty. It seemed the most natural thing in the world to be lying here naked in his arms. As he rid himself of the last vestige of his clothing, she reveled in the feel of skin against skin, still damp and cool from the river.

Tantalizing and teasing, he departed from her mouth as his tongue made a slow and sensuous exploration around the curve of her neck and up to the rosy tipped peak of first one breast and then the other. The effect was electric, and she gasped in pleasure, arching against him and drawing him closer. Instinctively she moved against him, her soft smooth skin connecting with his male hardness.

Grasping her hips firmly, he nibbled his way across her stomach, leaving her squirming as the tingles of pleasure danced across her belly. Moaning softly, Kathy was dimly aware that he was moving yet again.

With the assurance of rightful ownership, he lowered his head first to nuzzle the soft downy mound, then to plunder the sweet centre of pleasure which lay within. With warm waves of rippling sensation taking hold of her, Kathy abandoned herself to him entirely, enveloped in the symphony of pleasure he was orchestrating within her, coaxing to a crescendo that overwhelmed her with shuddering release. Acting instinctively, she drew him to her, anxious to be united, to feel him deep inside her. He eased himself upwards again, lips retracing the path over her belly and around the tips of her breasts. Her thighs parted in silent offering.

"Are you sure?" he whispered, raising himself so he could look into her eyes. "I'll stop if you want."

"I'm sure." Her whole body was sure.

Pausing a moment, he kissed her tenderly. She relaxed and reached out drawing him close. He began a slow and gentle rhythmic movement that became more abandoned as he gave himself up to the demanding sweet pleasure of her body.

Blissfully exhausted, they lay entwined, neither wanting to break the contact. For Kathy, it had been an unexpected transition. Now it had happened, she didn't want the connection to end, but she still needed time to process her emotions and responses. She ran her fingers gently up his back, feeling the knobbles of his backbone. Even that was a sensual experience. She relished the moment and the closeness.

"I didn't understand until too late that you've not… I mean… that you've not…

 Kathy laid a finger across his lips. "I didn't have the opportunity," she murmured, "but I didn't want you to stop. After a while, it didn't seem important."

He laughed softly, and nibbled on her ear, making her squeal and wriggle to get away from him. Finally, he sat up with a sigh.

"Well, my little water nymph. We'd better get back to Arapunya. If we don't hurry, they'll have a search and rescue party out looking for us."

The suggestion was enough to make her jump up in alarm. Dressing swiftly, Kathy looked around one last time with affection and regret. Tenderly, Alex kissed the top of her head before they both headed back to the plane. Neither of them looked back. Afternoons like that were better preserved in their memories.

They wasted no time in becoming airborne, and tracking in the direction of the Arapunya homestead. Hazy smoke still filled the air, but there were no immediate fires in their path. The heat of the day still sat heavily, and Kathy was aware of her heightened colour. *It's just the heat,* she told herself. But she knew her life had irrevocably changed. She hoped her face didn't reflect that for all to see and read. Conversation was minimal on the flight back, with each of them contained within their own thoughts and only routine radio broadcasts interrupting.

On touch down, a vehicle headed out to the strip and picked them up, driving them back to the schoolroom. Most of the others engaged in the day's program had already returned, and those who could to do so enjoyed an ice-cold beer. Cans raised in welcome from the clusters of people, engaged in convivial debrief, their laconic demeanour giving lie to the stressful events of the day.

"Oi, you two," one of the blokes called out. "What kept you so long? You'll have to be quick if you want a beer!"

Kathy waved in response and joined the group that was giving a run down on the day's activities and observations. The Commander greeted them with a curt nod and listened intently as they gave him their report. He recorded the salient details on the form on his clipboard.

"Good work you two. Well done! Get yourselves a cold drink—you've earned it. It's been bloody hot out there!"

You don't know the half of it. Kathy felt the flush creeping up her neck beneath the damp strands of hair that still clung to her face as she thought of the passion of those kisses, the sensation of his hands on her body, and the depth of what they had shared. She looked towards Alex, trying to gauge what he might be feeling or thinking at this moment but he was focused on a group who were discussing the day's events. A well-groomed figure pushed out from amongst them.

"Alex, what kept you so long? Everyone else has been back for ages!"

Melissa planted a possessive kiss firmly on his lips, and slipped her arm through his. "I hope you haven't forgotten we're having dinner at Plenty River tonight?"

She didn't say a word to Kathy. Didn't need to. Melissa was claiming her man. Humiliation overwhelmed her. She'd been such a fool. Kathy didn't wait to hear any more. Quickly gulping a glass of water and with brief farewells to the company in general, she beat a hasty retreat. She didn't look again at Alex who was in close conversation with Melissa. She didn't want to let him see the distress that must be written all over her face.

Removing the chocks, she prepared the aircraft for take-off. Applying full power, she knew her hand was shaking on the throttle. She felt sick to the very core. She should have known better. Bitter tears stung her eyes. He regarded her as one more notch on his belt; a novice available for conquest. She felt so stupid for allowing feelings for the man to develop to the point they had. If she never saw him again, it would be too soon! As she stared blindly ahead, a tear slowly made its way down her face, completing the picture of misery and despair.

CHAPTER 7

KATHY SHUT THE door behind her and kicked off her shoes, followed by her uniform. She tossed it into the laundry basket. It had been a long day, with a couple of passengers to drop off enroute as well as a full load of freight to sort and deliver to the various stations and outposts, and she was exhausted. The passengers were no trouble—quite the opposite but she didn't feel like making small talk. She had other things on her mind. The fires had subsided over the preceding week and were brought under control, but the flame raging inside her hadn't been dulled.

The shower went some way to easing the tensions and the heat of the day. Water pounding on her aching shoulder muscles had therapeutic benefits, followed by moisturiser rubbed all over her body afterwards. Sipping a cool drink, she checked the day's mail and thought about what she might cook for dinner. Salad and grilled fish perhaps? She ran through a list of tasks in her head. The washing needed to be brought in and tomorrow's uniform ironed and hung up ready to wear.

Kathy was still at the clothes line when she heard the phone ring from inside the unit.

Damn! Why does it always ring the moment I turn my back? She ran back inside, slamming the screen door behind her in the rush to grab the phone before it stopped ringing.

"Panting already? I wish I had that effect on all women."

She recognised the voice. Kathy clutched the phone tightly, her eyes widening as she took in what was said.

"Why did you take off so quickly last week? I thought you would at least have said goodbye. When I looked around, you were gone."

She hadn't expected the call. How could Alex sound so casual? No contact for a week and now this? A flush of anger engulfed her.

"I'm surprised you even noticed I was gone. You were otherwise engaged when I left."

"Otherwise engaged? What's that supposed to mean? Catching up with mates after a long hard day is hardly 'otherwise engaged' or whatever you want to call it."

"Perhaps I should clarify the situation for you. Whatever effect you have on other women, you don't have it on me. I regret what happened between us, and I'm determined it won't happen again." Her palm felt damp and clammy and she slipped the phone to the other hand before swiping the side of her jeans in lieu of a towel. She appeared prim, even to herself.

"You what?" Alex sounded incredulous. "You seemed happy at the time, or are you telling me you put on an act?"

"What I am saying is, you needn't bother calling me again. I'm sure you'll find lots of female company elsewhere. Try Plenty River for instance."

"Listen, Kathy..."

Kathy replaced the handset. She had never hung up on anyone before. She sat, staring at nothing in particular. The ache inside her, symptomatic of the feeling of malaise which had settled on her in recent days, intensified. She felt naïve and stupid—and embarrassed. Just a city girl—that's all she was to him. No one important. None of it had been important—not to Alex. Her eagerness in responding to his caresses was mortifying. That wouldn't happen again. Ever. Especially not without a condom. How could she have been so stupid?

Thoughts chased each other around and around until her head ached. Even a quiet drink on the veranda with Sarah did little to dispel her mood. By then the evening was softened by a breeze and the cicadas were singing their usual evening song.

"Long day, huh?"

"Mm. Something like that."

"I noticed you had some passengers on board. How were they?"

"Okay. Nice couple. Seemed to enjoy the flight. Not so much the heat and flies."

"Yeah—the heat's tiring for anybody, even us locals." Sarah pulled a wry face. "It can be draining after a while."

"You can say that again. I'm not sure I'll ever get used to the really intense heat."

Sarah screwed up her face with a look of concern. "You're not feeling homesick, are you?"

"Me? No, of course not."

"It's just that life in Alice is probably different to what you've experienced before. It must've been a culture shock— not just the heat, but everything. The distances, the dust, the flies and the long day— it's enough to drag anyone down, let alone someone who's new to it all."

"Look, I'm fine. Just tired, that's all."

Sarah didn't pursue her questions and they lapsed into a companionable silence. The evening didn't just bring in the mozzies and the chirping cicadas; Brian, Mark and Chris wandered over looking for a sundowner.

"Well, it's that time of day, isn't it?" declared Chris. "Who's joining me in a nice cold beer?"

"Yeah, I could sink a coldie—or perhaps two." Mark could always be relied on join a party. "I've been thinking of this all afternoon," he said, popping the ring top of a cold can and releasing a fine spray of icy mist. "Who else? Brian? Kathy, do you want a top up? Wash away the taste of the dust."

An old fridge was on the back porch, and it served as a drinks fridge for all the units. A shared kitty kept it stocked, but those who drank more tended to fill it up on their own initiative. Sarah helped herself to a gin and tonic, with the lemon tree in the back yard providing the zest but Kathy and Brian were happy with a can of soft drink each.

The break in temperature carried by the night air brought welcome relief, and Kathy turned her face upwards towards the cool of the breeze, welcoming the soothing effect on her skin. Inexplicably, Chris sighed and Mark renewed his efforts to impress her with his charm and wit.

When Brian rose to retire, Kathy followed suit. Smiling a quick good night, she slipped inside her flat, not wanting to impose her subdued mood on the others any longer.

"Got a moment, Kathy?"

Rob Collins held open the door to his office in an invitation for her to step inside. He nodded towards one of the visitor chairs facing his desk. Her mind raced back over recent weeks. *What have I done wrong? Has anyone made a complaint?*

Rob picked up a piece of paper on his desk, and peered at her over the top of his reading glasses.

"I had reports of your contribution to the team effort at Arapunya recently," he said, "and you seem to have ticked a few boxes with others in the company."

She nodded, hoping there weren't too many details about the team effort.

"As you know, you were engaged under a short-term contract. It still has a while to run, but I've reviewed the terms. We weren't offering a permanent role when we engaged you, as there were a few internal decisions to be made."

Kathy worked hard at maintaining a poker face. He must want to end the contract early. She had to be mature about this. Contract work was the nature of the industry. Something else would come along.

"I've consulted my co-directors, and it's a unanimous decision. We'd like to offer you a permanent position with StationAir. You don't have to give me your decision now. Take some time to think about it."

He handed her the piece of paper. "Here's the new Employment Agreement. If you decide to come on board permanently, sign it and drop it back to me. No rush. Tomorrow's fine."

He picked up his pen and began writing, with his attention now directed elsewhere. Kathy realised the discussion was over. She didn't need to think. The place had grown on her and so had the people; most of them anyway. She enjoyed her job. She had grown into it. What decision was there to be made? She reached over and picked up a pen. Signing the bottom, she left the document on his desk, shutting the door quietly as she left the room.

On collecting the post later that week, Kathy was surprised at the writing on an envelope. She would recognise Pete's scrawl anywhere. He wasn't known for writing; a quick phone call was usually his style. She loved receiving letters and this one, as she explained to Sarah later than night, brought welcome news.

"Pete hasn't been up this way in ages, but he's doing a delivery run, bringing a new Piper Warrior up to the Aero Club. He's taking a couple of days leave as well to spend some time in Alice before taking a commercial flight back home. It will be good to see him."

"Ah ha! Have you been holding out on me?" Sarah enquired. "Sounds like this Pete might be someone special? Wait until Chris and Mark hear about this."

"Don't get too excited. He was my instructor during my flight training and became a good friend. There's no more to it than that," she added firmly.

"Is that so?" Sarah's tone indicated a teasing disbelief.

With an exasperated flap of her hand, Kathy gave a potted history of her training days and the friendship that had followed.

"I got to know him quite well as I did most of my training with him. Being in such a confined space for so long, you can't help but get to know and understand each other. He had such a calm approach to his delivery. It made all the difference to my progress."

"So, you became close?" Sarah asked. "He must be keen if he wants to spend some time with you."

"Probably," Kathy conceded. "I'll enjoy having him around. He was in control before, but now he's coming into my territory." She paused, head to one side. "Do you know, I've learnt a lot since I've been in Alice. I feel like a pilot now, not just a raw recruit."

"Whatever the story, you're chirpier than I've seen you in ages," remarked Sarah. "What are your plans?"

"I'll be rostered on some of the time he's here, but I'll still be able to take him out to the Telegraph Station, and Wiggley's Waterhole and perhaps a couple of the local gorges. Maybe he could come with me on a mail run?" Kathy was in planning mode.

"Probably. Speak to Rob about it. I'm sure he won't mind."

"You're right. I wouldn't be surprised if he doesn't already know Pete. You know how incestuous the aviation community is. There are never more than a couple of degrees of separation."

Her anticipation grew over the following fortnight. Kathy hadn't realised how much she had missed Pete. She was keen to demonstrate how far she'd progressed since they first met. He was bringing with him the scent of home, and she did miss it from time to time. Sure, she loved her job and her new friends and the challenges, but there was a lot she had left behind too.

Kathy borrowed Sarah's car and drove to the airport to meet Pete. The day was clear—a brilliant example of Centralian weather, without being too hot for a change. He'd contacted her from his re-fuelling stop, so she knew when to expect him. Pulling up to the parking lot, she managed to find a shady area towards the rear. She locked the car and stood for a moment, squinting at the sky. There were aircraft in the circuit area in landing sequences, but none seemed to be the one she was waiting for. She strolled into the StationAir hangar and called Pete's aircraft from the hangar radio. Reception was really poor, especially with the noise of the aircraft in the background but she could still make out what he was saying. He expected to land in another fifteen minutes.

Filling in time, Kathy wandered towards the Aero Club hangar, where she planned to meet Pete. She heard the plane before she could see it. Squinting against the sun, she finally made out the small shape, and watched as it grew larger, then descended to circuit level, joining the downwind leg. She could hear the radio broadcasts being relayed through the speaker installed on the external wall of the club rooms and Pete was cleared to land.

Several cars sat in the car park adjacent to the club house, and she could make out the silhouettes of people seated in the lounge area. The anti-glare tinting on the glass made it difficult to see clearly from outside. Still, as the plane was taxiing in, Kathy saw that Alex Woodleigh sat in the lounge area with several others. *Damn. He's bound to see me here. Of all the horrible coincidences…*

The small aircraft left the runway and turned onto the taxiway that led towards the general aviation area. Kathy gave a huge wave and could see a corresponding movement through the tinted screen that she took to be a wave in return. Pete manoeuvred the plane into the parking position, and shut down the engine. Kathy raced across to greet him as he clambered out of the cockpit.

"Pete! It's good to see you. How was the trip? You must be so stiff after such a long flight!"

He grabbed her in a big bear hug. "All the better for seeing you. My goodness you've got a bit of a tan. It looks like all this fresh air has been doing you good." He held her at arm's length, looking her up and down. "Whatever you've been doing up here, it agrees with you." He clasped her to him in another hug. "I've looked forward to this. The trip was long, but worth it."

Kathy grinned at the compliment, and took a cheerful delight in the knowledge this little reunion would have been witnessed through the windows of the Club house. *Up yours, Alex Woodleigh. There are people in my life who really appreciate me.* It wasn't pretence. She really was glad to see Pete.

She kept up an exuberant chat as he tied the aircraft down and walked over to the club rooms to deliver the paperwork and keys to the Club Manager.

"Do you expect to be long?" she asked.

"Not really. There are no problems to report. I'll just get a signature acknowledging safe delivery."

"Okay. I won't come in. I'll pop into the StationAir office two hangars down to check on a couple of things. See you back here in ten."

When she returned, Pete was not quite finished but she waited outside, preferring the shade of a tree to the heat from the company in the clubroom.

First stop was the motel so that Pete could check in and have a quick shower. He wanted to cool down and freshen up. Kathy chose to take a drink out to sit by the pool while she waited.

She kicked off her shoes and flexed her toes in the cool grass. *I could get used to this. I've been so focused on work since I arrived in Alice. I haven't had much 'me' time. It's just as well Pete made this trip. It's made me take a step back.*

She had dozed off by the time Pete emerged from his room. Either he made a slight noise or she sensed that she was being watched as her eyes suddenly sprang open.

She stretched languorously. "All refreshed? It has been lovely out here. I haven't relaxed like this in ages." She eased herself out of the poolside chair. "If you're ready, we can make a move. Grab a jacket. I know it's hot now, but the temperature can be cool after the sun goes down."

A barbecue with the StationAir crew waited for them back at the flats, but first she took him to the top of Anzac Hill. Dusk was still some time off, but still, there was the view over the township and the majesty of the MacDonnell Ranges to the rear.

"Sarah brought me here that first day when she picked me up from the train. It was a brilliant introduction to the town, and since then I've come up here a few times when I just felt like some time out. I love the view."

"Wow—it really puts the town into perspective. I can see Heavitree Gap in the distance, and what's that over there?"

Kathy pointed out the salient features and he stood reflectively, absorbing it all.

"After the arid country that I flew over earlier today, this is like an oasis. Dusty perhaps, but still a contrast."

"We don't have the time to wait today, but when twilight falls, the colours over the Ranges as viewed from up here are quite magical. I'm glad Sarah introduced me to this spot."

"Magical? I'm not sure I could ever view the Alice in that light. It must be your romantic streak, Kathy."

His tone was slightly dismissive and Kathy felt a pang of disappointment. She so wanted him to understand the emotions the site engendered in her, but didn't say anything else. Still, he'd had a long day and was probably tired.

"We'd better be going. The others will be wondering where we are."

By the time they pulled up, Mark and Chris were organizing the barbecue and Brian was setting up the garden furniture and umbrella. Sarah supervised.

"Not there. The sun will be in our eyes. Have you cleaned that table? Chris, isn't that flame too hot? We want barbecued, not grilled to a crisp!"

The men rolled their eyes good naturedly. They all turned to greet the newcomers. Mark had tongs in one hand, a can of beer in the other. He raised the can in greeting.

"G'day mate. Mark's the name. Welcome to Chez Nous. Can't shake; I'm somewhat occupied here."

Kathy continued the introductions and there were handshakes and words of welcome all round.

"Like a beer, Pete?" Brian inquired.

"I thought you'd never ask. It's been a dry, hot day, for sure."

They settled into the serious business of cooking, sorting out the salads and lighting mosquito coils. Kathy took care of the music, bringing the speakers outside and deciding which albums to play. Pete filled them in on the details of his flight. The evening passed with the usual bonhomie, self-indulgence, and tall stories that accompany gatherings of pilots. Kathy also gave them an outline of her plans for Pete over the next few days and the others either indicated a seal of approval or else gave her a few tips and hints. It gave Pete an insight into the camaraderie that Kathy spoke of so highly.

The next few days passed in a whirl of activity. Kathy took Pete with her on the same mail run on which Brian had accompanied her when she first arrived in Alice. She felt like an old hand as she showed him the country, pointing out the local features from the air and introducing him to the locals.

They passed the Elkedra River, and she dropped low so that he could get a better view. The day was hotter than her first visit and so the river was drier but there were still some waterholes and the birdlife was evident. She didn't mention the waterhole where she had swum. She tried not to even think about it.

They met Bob at Bundy Station, only on this occasion he was far more relaxed with Kathy and they shared a quick cuppa and a biscuit with him before setting off again. In anticipation of this, Kathy had brought with her a tin of Anzac Biscuits. She knew now they were Bob's favourites.

Mulga Downs was also on the run. Kathy hoped Alex would not be at the airstrip, reasoning he would have heard her inbound calls on the radio. Surely, he would have the sense to send someone else to meet them. Perhaps even Rose would come down. Some hope. As she taxied up to the parking area, a figure unwound itself from the cabin of the vehicle parked in the shade and she knew immediately it was Alex. There he stood, hands on hips as she drew to a halt, and cut the engine. She busied herself with sorting out the luggage compartment and the mail bag, and Pete strode over to the waiting figure, hand extended.

"G'day. Nice place you've got here. I'm Pete Thompson—just along for the ride today." Pete looked around with interest. Alex hesitated momentarily, and then shook the extended hand.

"Thanks. We try." He looked in Kathy's direction. "How are you, Kathy? Nice for you to have company today."

"Yes." She kept her eyes on a point just past his shoulder to avoid looking directly at him. Why didn't he just grab the mail bag and go? She handed it over and nearly jumped when his hand brushed against hers.

"Nice day for it," he added. "Especially if you're planning on cooling off with a swim."

His comment shocked her into looking at him, but his expression was unreadable—until one eyebrow lifted sardonically. She quickly looked away.

"Pete, if you're ready, we've a schedule to keep. We should keep going." She shut the luggage compartment door and moved around to her side of the cabin. She didn't acknowledge Alex in any way again. Pete gave a half salute in farewell and climbed in also.

"Strange sort of bloke," he commented as they commenced their take-off roll. "Not very communicative, was he?" Kathy snorted in response, but had no inclination to discuss the encounter further.

On the first of her days off, she borrowed Gordon and they explored the local scenic spots. They visited Emily and Jessie Gorge and then had a picnic lunch at the Old Telegraph Station, looking over the old buildings and learning about the town's history. In the early days of settlement, it was an important relay point for telegraphic communications between Adelaide and Darwin. Later, it became a home for Aboriginal children who had been removed from their families by the authorities of the day.

"How awful," said Kathy. "Can you imagine the anguish of those mothers and then the confusion of the children, being taken from the life they knew? It doesn't bear thinking about."

Pete was pragmatic. "Well, we think it's awful now—and of course it was—but at the time, the authorities thought they were acting in the best interests of those children. They thought they were protecting them."

"I know that's what they thought, but it's difficult to understand how they could be so arrogant and lacking in empathy."

"Ah Kathy," he said throwing an arm protectively around her shoulders. You're such a sensitive soul about so many things. Perhaps you need someone to protect you from some of life's harsh realities."

Kathy shrugged uncomfortably and moved forward so Pete's arm fell away. "If your lunch has settled, we could do the scenic walk to Trigg Hill. It'll give us some exercise." In her heart, she knew the conversation was heading in a direction she didn't want. She preferred to keep moving.

The next day, Kathy hired a Piper Warrior from the Aero Club, and they flew down to Uluru, taking in Kings Canyon from the air on the way. Kathy flew down and Pete navigated and, on their return, they swapped roles. They fell into the old partnership they had developed during her training days, with each anticipating what the other's next action or request would be. The weather was mild and the air was crystal clear. They could see for miles. From Uluru, they took a local tour around the base of the Rock and then out to Kata Tjuta, otherwise known by the European name of The Olgas. The view through the Valley of the Winds was breathtaking and they were glad they had decided to take the tour.

By the time they touched down back in Alice, they were exhausted but Kathy was in an elated mood. They were so lucky, she thought, to be able to just hire a plane and fly over such unique and fabulous scenery and the day together had gone really well. The changing colours and vegetation challenged her concept of outback Australia. Once, she had thought the middle of the continent was just desert, but that wasn't true. They even saw a herd of wild brumbies, and a short time later a couple of camels at a waterhole.

She was glad she'd spent such a fantastic day with Pete. They tied the aircraft down, and checked in with the Club. A few members were having a sundowner in the lounge area, and on impulse Pete and Kathy joined them, regaling the others with descriptions of what they had seen and done. Bruce couldn't resist giving Pete a run down on Kathy's flour-bombing efforts.

The next day was Pete's last in Alice. Kathy was rostered on, and Pete could have accompanied her, but he opted to do some local sightseeing, checking out the galleries and going for a walk. They agreed they should go out for dinner in final celebration of his visit.

"Kathy, this one's on me. You've done so much for me over these few days and have gone to such a lot of trouble. I'll say goodbye to all the others of course, but tomorrow should be just us. Where do you recommend?"

"Well, there is a restaurant at your motel, but it would be nice on your last night to see a little more of what the town has to offer. What about Martines? Sarah has mentioned it a few times and said the food and service were really good."

Pete smiled. "I'll leave the choice in your hands. You know the town better than I do."

"If you're looking for some bush tucker, I think they serve kangaroo and emu dishes, or there are more traditional options available. I'll come to your motel first, and we can walk together from there."

"Then it's a date. You're probably tired after our long day today, so I won't come back to the flats with you. I might have an early night myself."

"You're right. I do need to get a few things ready for tomorrow." With a quick farewell peck on the cheek, she headed for home, accompanied by her own thoughts. She didn't linger when she returned the car keys to Sarah, wanting to kick off her shoes and to chill for a while in her own space.

Sipping her cup of tea, Kathy mentally reviewed the days past. It had been great seeing Pete again. He was a good friend and always would be. She knew he was attracted to her, but the distance between them that recent months had imposed had affirmed her view she would never be drawn to him in any romantic sense. Just little things that he had said or done during this visit had reinforced that understanding. They shared a love of aviation but some of their values and approaches to life were quite different.

Anyway, following recent events she didn't particularly want to be too close to any man. What was the point? She was better off leading her own life and developing her career. All the same, she was regretful that Pete's visit was almost over.

There hadn't been many opportunities for dining out since her arrival in Alice. Kathy considered the various options in her wardrobe, before settling on a soft ruffled dress of bluey-green patterns, with a halter neckline that showed off the elegance of her neck and her tanned shoulders. She even put her hair up for a change, though wispy bits insisted on escaping and curling around the side of her face. Some eye-shadow, a hint of lipstick and the addition of a Swarovski Crystal necklace, and she was ready.

Pete was impressed when she arrived at his motel. He was even *very* impressed.

"Kathy, you look absolutely stunning. The colour you've picked up since coming here suits and that dress looks fabulous on you."

She blushed and laughed. "I don't have much opportunity to dress up. It makes a welcome change to get out of my uniform or alternatively casual clothes."

She gave a twirl so that the dress fanned out around her, laughing as she did.

"Come on; we're walking to the restaurant, don't forget."

The restaurant was in an old house that had been converted for the new purpose. Some of the internal walls had been removed to make a larger dining space, with some smaller rooms retained to create private dining areas. They weren't in a private room but were in a small alcove set to one side, giving them privacy but the ability to observe the other diners. Inevitably, Kathy saw a couple of familiar faces. She noted the curious glances as they first caught sight of her and Pete. She sighed. She already knew there were no secrets in a small town and what people didn't know, they would assume anyway.

If there had been a *Martine* once, she was not in evidence any more. The photographs on the wall depicted the early history of the house from when it had been an early family home, built by a local dignitary but there was nothing of the enigmatic namesake. They pondered the question during a pre-dinner drink—champagne for Kathy and light ale for Pete.

The meal and the service were good, and to their surprise there was even a local wine that was quite drinkable. Somehow, they had not considered that the Centre could accommodate vineyards as well. They were more engrossed in conversation though rather than the meal.

"Here's to us Kathy," said Pete raising his glass. "Thank you for a wonderful few days. It's gone too quickly but I've enjoyed every moment." They clinked glasses and Kathy smiled but was reluctant to hold his gaze.

"Pete, it's been a delight to have you here," she said. "I was pleased I could show you the sights, and of course to catch up on all the news from Adelaide. I get snippets from the old gang, but it's not the same as hearing the details in person."

"Well, if you came back to Adelaide sometime, you could catch up with everyone for yourself." Kathy was playing with the stem of her wine glass and Pete reached across to take her hand. "You know we'd all love to see you. Perhaps after you have gained more experience up here, you can apply for a job back in Adelaide. I've mentioned it before, but you could do your instructor rating and work at the flying school."

Kathy freed her hand to take a sip of wine, being careful not to place her hand back on the table. "Pete, I don't think I have the patience for instructing. For now, I love my work here and perhaps in time I could look at joining a regional airline. I need a lot more flying hours under my belt before I can consider that option though."

"Well, think about it. Perhaps you could come down over the next long weekend? The break would do you good."

Kathy smiled and said "Perhaps" but was non-committal beyond that and Pete let the matter drop. Only after they had reached the coffee stage, with a complimentary truffle did he mentioned the photos. "Speaking of Adelaide, I meant to show you the photos I have of you and those who trained with you. Some were taken on the day of the air show and others were at different stages of training. I got double copies of the prints and brought up a set for you but left them in my room. If you walk back to the motel with me, I'll give them to you."

"Great. That will be a fantastic memento. I didn't take many photos of that time. I meant to but then got absorbed in the moment and just forgot. It's thoughtful of you to bring them."

"Would've been tragic if I hadn't remembered I had them. Come on. I'll fix up the bill and we can wander back to the motel."

The hot day had dissolved into a clear evening that was refreshingly mild. Frangipani trees grew in the streets, and the sweet heady scent floated on the breeze. She'd always thought it hinted at romance, but this was one occasion on which she was not romantically inclined.

The motel was only a couple of streets away. Just as well, given her strappy shoes were not meant for walking.

"My room's upstairs. Come up with me while I retrieve the packet from my bag—or is it in my flying case?" He pondered the matter and shrugged. "No matter, I'll find it. I'll just get my key from reception."

Kathy wandered towards the stairs while Pete waited for attention at the desk. A group of people left the motel restaurant, which also opened into the foyer. Kathy glanced over, only to freeze in horror. Alex and a party of people were leaving the restaurant. *Please,* she thought. *Please, please don't look this way.* Perhaps if she kept really still, he wouldn't notice her.

No such luck. With stony look, he took in the scenario instantly—Kathy poised by the staircase that led to the guest rooms, and Pete collecting his room key. Alex moved closer, his eyes raking her derisively.

"Well, some people are fast learners! Making up for lost time?" His insolent drawl was pitched low enough for only Kathy to hear.

"The only time I consider a loss is the time that I have spent with you!" she hissed, and without waiting for further reply, turned and ran up the stairs.

"Kathy, wait, I'm coming!" called Pete as he hastened up after her, oblivious to the steely pair of eyes that followed him.

CHAPTER 8

MARY'S NURSING HOME was easy to find. There was only one in Alice. Keeping in mind her promise to Tom, Kathy used a rostered day off to visit and introduce herself. She presented herself at the reception desk

"Can you tell me where to find Mary Daly? I'm visiting her today."

"The woman on reception looked up and smiled.

"Mary loves visitors. She'll be glad to see you. I think she might be out in the garden. She likes to get out in the fresh air. Follow me. I'll take you out there."

The receptionist led the way through a common room and out through a set of double doors. A woman sat in a wheel chair in the shade of a tree, listening to Classic FM on the radio.

"Mary—there's a young lady here to see you."

The woman spoke loudly and slowly, and Kathy thought she saw Mary wince.

"Melissa? Is that Melissa?"

That was a surprise. Who would have thought Melissa visited?

"No Mary, I'm Kathy. I fly for StationAir and met your husband, Tom."

The receptionist gave Kathy a quick nod and a smile. "I'll leave you to it." She disappeared back through the double doors, leaving Kathy standing uncertainly. Was this a good idea?

She moved closer and put herself in Mary's field of vision. The elderly woman was slumped to one side, her hands and occasionally her whole body trembling. Her eyes though were curious. She attempted a smile.

"T-T-Tom t-told me about you."

Looking around, Kathy spied a garden setting. She fetched one of the chairs and placed it close to Mary so they were on the same level.

"We had the annual fly-in out at Jinka recently. I took a few photos and thought you might like to see them."

Mary blinked her agreement. The photos broke the ice. Her speech was tremulous, but she recognised many of the people featured in the photos and took her time looking at each one. Occasionally, she pointed at different people or depicted scenes, and Kathy understood that more explanation was required.

Mary had difficulty speaking coherently, and she became embarrassed when she was not easily understood. With nods, gestures and goodwill, they managed to have a conversation. Kathy also found that the more she listened, the easier to comprehend what Mary tried to say.

"I'll come back and see you again, if you like Mary? Can I bring you something to read?

143

Mary shook her head decisively.

"Talking books? I can get those from the library, or music cassettes." This suggestion got a shaky thumbs up.

She was in the process of taking her leave, when the receptionist called from the doorway.

"You're popular today, Mary. You've another visitor."

Alex was standing behind her, carrying a bulky bag. The woman, having done what was required, disappeared again, leaving Kathy and Alex to stare at each other.

"A-a-lex," Mary called out, looking visibly pleased to see him.

Kathy turned back to Mary. "I'll leave you to your next visitor, Mary. I'll see you on my next day off."

"You needn't go because of me," Alex said curtly. "I'm only dropping something off from mum."

"I was just going anyway. Mary and I have already had a lengthy chat."

She avoided his gaze, but as she left, could feel his eyes boring into her back. She couldn't get out of there fast enough. It took a while for the adrenaline surge to settle. That man had an uncanny knack of pushing her buttons.

A few weeks after Pete's visit, Kathy's mother tentatively asked, during a Sunday phone call with her parents that if it would be convenient to her if they came up for a visit.

"We saw that friend of yours Kathy—what's his name? Peter. We were at the supermarket and he recognised us. After he approached us, I realised who he was; that nice instructor of yours. He dropped you off here after training and stayed for a meal on a couple of occasions. A very polite young man."

"Oh. That was nice, Mum."

"He told us all about his trip to Alice and how much he enjoyed it. He dropped around later and showed us the photos he took and it got us thinking. Would you mind if Dad and I came up for a visit? We thought we might fly up and then take a coach back, seeing some of the country and detouring past Uluru on the way."

"Mum, I'd love to see you both. If I can wrangle it, I'll take you on some local flights. There is so much to see. You and Dad can have my bed and I'll sleep on the sofa bed. When are you thinking of coming?"

"We don't want to put you out at all, love. We can stay at a motel."

"Don't be silly. If you want the convenience of the motel, that's fine but I can easily put you up—honestly. It will give you a chance to meet everybody."

"If you're sure it won't be a bother to you, we'll book in about four weeks' time. That will give us time to get organized and arrange for someone to look after the house while we're away."

Kathy was delighted. She knew her parents had harboured the idea of visiting her ever since she first got the job, and as Sarah had warned her—anyone living in a town imbued with as much mystique as Alice Springs always has a stream of visitors. The others joked about her new career as a tour guide, but it seemed various family members had visited them at different times as well.

The next four weeks went quickly. Once again, Kathy prevailed upon Sarah to borrow the car, stressing she would fill it up with petrol.

"Why don't I drive out to the airport with you?" asked Sarah. "That way, you'll be free to talk to your parents and can point out places of interest on our way back into town."

"It's a great idea, but I don't want to impose on you. I have to warn you—my mother can talk a lot!"

"You won't be putting me out and I'm sure that I can handle a talkative mother. I might even enjoy it. I could hear all sorts of stories about you."

This last comment was made with a laugh punctuated with a wink. Kathy reflected how lucky she was to have such a good friend, even one who teased.

The aircraft had barely shut down the engines before the stairs were wheeled into place. No aerobridge for a town like Alice. A short hot walk led across the tarmac to the gate opening onto the grassed viewing area in front of the terminal building. This was where Kathy waited, eager for her first view of her parents as they emerged at the top of the stairs.

She spotted them as they crossed the tarmac. Her father, the taller of the two had thick hair that had gone prematurely white. It gave him a distinguished air, much to the chagrin of her mother who said it wasn't fair. If a woman went prematurely white, she was assumed to be old. Her mother was an attractive woman though. She dressed smartly and was always impeccably groomed. Soft golden waves framed her face, thanks to the hairdresser who was responsible for the colour tones. She had a wonderful smile that lit up her face and instantly drew people to her. Kathy had inherited that feature from her mother.

Kathy could see they weren't alone. Her mother was deep in conversation while her father followed behind, carrying the hand luggage. To her amazement, she realised her mother was talking to Rose Woodleigh. How did that come about? Kathy waved and her mother, scanning the waiting crowd, recognised her and waved back.

"Kathy!" her mother said when they were finally able to embrace. "Have you lost weight? You're looking so tanned. What have you been eating? You look different!"

"Mum, you sure haven't changed. I'm fine as you can see. Dad, it's so good to see you." She had a hug for her father as well. Their greeting was intense and emotional.

Kathy's mother finally pulled away from the embrace, and turned to the woman alongside her, who was still scanning the meeters and greeters.

"Kathy, I believe you already know Rose. We sat next to each other on the plane. Our take-off was delayed in Adelaide for some reason and we got talking while we waited."

"Hello Kathy. It's lovely to see you again. I've had such an interesting chat to your mother. We have quite a few things in common".

Rose looked around her in the terminal, obviously looking for someone.

"I wonder where that boy of mine is!"

"Boy? Oh, you mean Alex?"

"Yes dear, he was supposed to meet me. I guess he'll be here soon."

"Umm yes, I suppose so." Kathy twisted around, spotting Sarah standing back a respectful distance. "Sarah, come and meet my parents." The turned to watch as the young woman approached.

"Sarah met me when I first arrived in Alice, and helped me settle in. I would have been absolutely lost without her. Sarah, these are my parents, Judy and Robert Sullivan."

"Sarah, I've heard so much about you—let me give you a hug too." Judy Sullivan swept Sarah into a warm embrace. Rose and Sarah also exchanged greetings

Rose followed them through the terminal building and they all wandered over to the area where the luggage was delivered. While Kathy assisted her parents to identify and retrieve their suitcases, Sarah went to get the car, intending to swing past the terminal building and pick up both her passengers and the luggage. As she drew to a halt in front of them, Rose was still scanning the arriving vehicles, anxiously by this stage.

"Where do you need to go, Rose?" asked Kathy.

"Just to the townhouse, dear. I'll stay there tonight and go home to Mulga Downs in the morning. I have a few things to do in town anyway and some shopping too."

"Well, we could drop you off there," said Kathy. "Would that be okay Sarah? We have the station wagon. We can fit the luggage in the rear compartment.

"I don't want to put you to any trouble," Rose said as she scanned the forecourt again.

"No trouble at all. It will be on our way. Dad, you sit in front with Sarah—you'll have more room there for your legs and the rest of us will sit on the back."

She noticed Rose still scanning the approaching cars. Waiting for someone who was late was disconcerting. Had they forgotten? Had there been an accident?

"Have you tried calling Alex, Rose? If you don't catch him, leave a message to say that you're getting a lift into town."

Rose tried to call Alex from the public phone in the terminal building. There was no answer, so as Kathy suggested, she left a message advising Alex what she was doing. That taken care of, they piled into the car. With a wave to the Security Officer, who had to keep traffic moving, Sarah pulled out and followed the road that led into Alice. Kathy pointed out various features along the way, with Sarah chiming in as well. As they drove through Heavitree Gap, the extremities of the township were revealed on the other side. Kathy's parents were impressed by the breadth of the Todd River, its sandy bed dotted with pools of water at the base of stately gum trees.

"Does the water ever flow?" Bob inquired.

"It certainly does," Rose replied. "Comes down in a torrent and washes away everything in its path —vehicles, people, whatever. I don't think that it will happen on this visit. The Gap has significance to the local Aboriginal people, but the recent inhabitants of the town have muscled in with their road and the railway so in an industrial way it has desecrated the place."

They observed the river in reflective silence. Sarah caught Rose's eye in the rear vision mirror.

"Umm—Rose? You'll have to direct me from here. I'm not sure where your town house is."

"Turn left here, please." Rose continued the directions until they pulled up in front of the house that the family used when they stayed in town. The bungalow had wide verandas and a native garden; suitable given it needed to be self-sustaining. A round white metal table and two chairs sat on the front veranda, perhaps an ideal spot to sit in the early morning sun and have a cup of tea or coffee. The house looked well-kept, considering Rose was only occasionally in residence.

"Thank you so much for the lift, Sarah," Rose said. "I appreciate it. Something must have held Alex up. Now, you must all come in for a cup of tea or coffee."

"Rose, we don't want to put you out. You've only just arrived home."

"Nonsense. It will be no trouble at all. Besides, I want to show your mother a quilt that I told her about on the flight up."

Both women shared an interest in quilting, and as her mother made moves to get out of the car, Kathy realised the matter was settled. She exchanged a bemused glance with her father, in acknowledgement that they had little say in the matter. Once quilting was being discussed, that was that.

Rose bustled about with the kettle and the makings of tea and coffee, and told them a little about her visit to her sister in Adelaide.

"Rose," Sarah exclaimed, "we forgot your luggage in the back of the car. Kathy and I'll go and get it."

"Goodness. I was so happy to have guests I didn't give it another thought. Thank you—that would be helpful if you could bring it inside. There are wheels on the suitcase so you don't need to carry it. I did some shopping so it might be heavy."

She called this last comment after them as they bustled out the door with a quick smile at each other. Of course, she would have done some shopping. Just as they would if they visited a big city again! They were manoeuvring the luggage out of the car when, with a cloud of dust, Alex pulled up into the driveway.

"What are you two doing here?"

"Well hello to you too." Sarah tossed her curls. "Seeing as you abandoned your mother at the airport, we gave her a lift into town. She's making a cup of coffee for Kathy's parents at the moment."

"Is she indeed?" He made for the front door then abruptly stopped and came back again. He attempted to take the suitcase from Kathy. "I'll take that."

"I'm fine. I can manage." She kept her hold on the handle.

"I've no doubt you can manage, but I'll take it." There was a brief tussle before Kathy let go. She glared after him as he marched ahead into the house.

"It's just a suitcase, Kathy," murmured Sarah. "If he wants to make a show of manly strength, let him take it. Better he strains his back than you do."

She and Kathy trailed behind, entering in time to see the wayward son give his mother a huge hug with apologies.

"Sorry Mum. I had a flat tyre on the way into town, and was already running late. It was just one of those days."

"Sarah was able to give me a lift into town. You know Sarah, don't you?"

He nodded in Sarah's direction. "Sure do. Thanks for bringing Mum in," he said. "I owe you one."

Sarah gave him one of her usual cheeky grins. "No problems. Couldn't leave Rose stranded there, could I? I guess it makes up for helping us with the tyre on the way to Harts Ranges."

"I wasn't expecting payment in kind for that. It was the least I could do under the circumstances."

Kathy noted that he smiled at Sarah. It shouldn't have bothered her but it did. The fact exacerbated her fast-diminishing mood.

"Well, now that you're here Alex," said Rose, "you'd better have a cup of tea. Sit yourself down."

He did, focusing on the tea and the biscuits that Rose produced from the cupboard.

The three parents engaged in easy conversation, talking about life in Alice and then again out on Mulga Downs. Bob attempted to draw Alex into the conversation too, asking questions about the property—how big was it, what sort of cattle did they run and that sort of thing.

"Sounds like you've got your work cut out for you with a property that size, but I suppose you have people working for you?"

"I do. It's too much work for just me, depending on the time of year and what's happening on the property. There are a couple of blokes who live there full time, and then others who are employed on a contract basis when needed."

"Ah, well, that makes sense. Have you been out there Kathy?"

"Yes. Mulga Downs is a stop-off point on one of the mail routes. I get there on a regular basis—to the airstrip anyway."

"So, you haven't seen the station operations?"

"Only in passing. I've seen enough generally to know what goes on. I don't have much time to stop. I usually have quite a list of pick-ups and deliveries, sometimes with passengers, so I have to keep to schedule."

"Yes of course," said Bob. "I seem to recall that I couldn't entice you out into my vegie garden in Adelaide, so I don't suppose you're going to have an interest in a huge property like that."

There was a snorting sound. "Sorry," said Alex. "My tea went down the wrong way."

He avoided making eye contact with anyone, staring into the cup and the tea that he had slopped into the saucer. Kathy glared at him. He was laughing at her.

"I've picked up some local knowledge since I've been here, Dad, and I'm always happy to take the opportunity to learn more. I've even had an introduction to some of the edible bush plants and it was… fascinating." The frost in her tone indicated it had been anything but.

Rose turned to Bob and Judy. "You must have been a little dismayed when Kathy got a job so far away from you both."

"It was a wrench for us," said Judy, "but we knew when she started her training that the job could take her anywhere."

"We hadn't thought she would end up in Alice Springs," added Bob. "We've never been up this way before, so it has given us the perfect excuse to visit now. We get to see our daughter and to explore the Centre at the same time. Looking from the plane window at the country below was amazing, so now I'm keen to see it in greater detail." Bob munched his biscuit in quiet reflection and his wife took over.

"We saw some wonderful photos that Kathy's friend Pete brought back from Alice on his recent visit, and that decided us. We just had to come and have a look for ourselves. And see Kathy of course." Judy smiled at her daughter. "We've missed her. She's our baby you know. Came a few years after the others."

Kathy rolled her eyes. *Mum do you really have to? You make it sound as though I'm five years old.*

Alex had said little until this point, but he now joined the conversation. "This Pete," he inquired mildly. "He was a friend of the family, was he?"

"Well, a friend of Kathy's really. He was her instructor when she was training." Judy turned to Alex. "He would often either pick her up or drop her off when they had an early or late training session. We got quite used to him dropping in from time to time, didn't we Bob? Particularly at meal times but that's fine. There's always room for one more at our table."

Rose nodded her appreciation of that philosophy. "I certainly understand that scenario."

The two women exchanged complicit smiles before Judy continued.

"I ran into Pete shortly after his trip to Alice and he told me all about it. Well, not all of it then. Pete knew that we would be interested in the photographs he had taken, and so he dropped around one evening to show them to us."

"Actually," broke in Kathy, anxious to make a point while the opportunity was there, "Pete is quite a good friend. I enjoyed his visit and really missed him when he left."

She avoided looking at Alex. She did note the quizzical look on Sarah's face and quickly averted her eyes from her also. She knew she had not given Sarah an impression of a pining heart in recent weeks.

"Well, I don't know Kathy," interrupted her father. "If that's the way you feel, you should tell Pete that! The poor man was quite disconsolate when he was talking to me.

Seemed to think that you weren't really interested. You shouldn't be such a tease."

Kathy blushed. She could feel Alex's eyes upon her, his look one of scornful disbelief. Why didn't her father know when to keep quiet?

She was grateful when Sarah jumped in with a change in conversation, talking about the upcoming Camel Races that were held every year.

Her relief was short-lived. Rose suggested that it would be lovely if Kathy's parents were able to visit her on Mulga Downs.

"You could stay for a couple of days. It would give you an opportunity to see another facet of life in the Centre, and I'd love to have some visitors. I get sick of my own company sometimes. Bob, seeing as you're interested in the running of the property, I am sure you could accompany Alex for a while. You're welcome to do that as well Judy, though I warn you that the station vehicles are usually covered in dust. That would be all right, wouldn't it Alex?"

"Sure—not a problem. I have to come back into town at the end of the week and I can pick them up and fly them out there when I've finished with my business here."

"That would be wonderful," enthused Bob. "I'd like to get a closer look at what you do, as long as it's no trouble."

"No trouble at all. I'm not sure when I could bring you back, though."

"That's easy," said Sarah. "Kathy and I could drive out on Sunday and pick you up," said Sarah. "I haven't been for a decent drive in ages."

"Then that's settled," said Rose. "You girls should arrive late morning so we can all have lunch together before you head back to Alice."

Kathy tried to think of a good excuse why her parents shouldn't go, but realised that she couldn't say anything without sounding surly and childish. She knew her parents would thoroughly enjoy the trip, and it would put some life into the letters that she had written home. Their visit didn't have to involve close interaction between her and Alex. In fact, she would make sure that it didn't.

Not wanting to overstay their welcome, and conscious that Rose had things to do, the group made noises about leaving.

"Give me your phone number, Kathy," said Rose. "I'll put it in my address book now in case I need to contact you. Where is my book?" She rummaged through her handbag without success. "When did I last have it? I know—when I was about to ring you, Alex. I must have left it on the back seat of the car. Be a dear and go and get it for me, will you?"

Well, Kathy thought as Alex headed for the front door. *At least he responds when his mother speaks to him.*

Sarah waved her car keys in the air. "He might have a problem getting in, as I locked the doors after we took the suitcase out."

"Quick Kathy," said Judy, "take the keys out to him."

"Sarah's got the car keys mum. She'll take them out."

"Here, Kathy. I want to finish my cup of tea before we go. You take them."

Kathy was quietly furious but what could she do? Sarah sat there, a picture of innocence and wearing a wicked smile.

Kathy snatched the keys and followed Alex out to the car. He was already trying the car doors.

"You might need these." Kathy held out the keys.

"Thanks." As she turned to go, his voice abruptly halted her. "So, this Pete's only a good friend, is he? Looked more than that to me, or are you just a good actress? Seems you make a habit of being a tease."

"My relationship with Pete has nothing to do with you."

"I guess you're right. Nor your relationship with Brian, or Chris or Mark—nice blokes all of them. Have you led them on as well?" His voice was deceptively soft. "That little miss innocent is all a put on, isn't it? You're like a cat that plays with its prey. Well watch out you don't find yourself in a trap of your own one day."

"You're a fine one to talk. If you're threatening me, I'm not impressed."

"Sweetheart, I wouldn't bother." He reached out an insolent finger, tilting her chin upwards. "You'll sink yourself without any help from me." Before she could jerk away, he swiftly reached forward and planted a quick kiss on her parted lips. "Did you know your eyes glitter when you're angry?"

Without waiting for a reply, he unlocked the car and retrieved the book from the seat. He strode back into the house, passing Sarah on the way.

"Well, that was a touching little scene. You were gone so long, I wondered if there was a problem, but it looks to me you were doing just fine. Kathy Sullivan, what have you been keeping from me?"

"Don't be silly! There's absolutely nothing to tell."

"Oh, no?"

"Look, here come my parents. I can't talk about this now."

"Okay, but later I want the goss… every last detail."

The next couple of hours were spent on a quick drive through the town, noting key features, and then back to the flats. Bob and Judy had agreed they would stay with Kathy instead of a motel. The evening meal, which Kathy had thought to prepare in advance, was followed by gin and tonics on the veranda, until the mozzies forced them inside.

Later, while Bob and Judy were watching the evening news on television, Kathy popped around to see Sarah in her flat. It was a relief in a way to be able to tell someone about what had been happening, leaving out some of the more intimate detail. She stuck to the salient points, finishing with a description of what happened at the end of the fire spotting flight, when Alex had abandoned her for Melissa.

"Sarah, I know I'm going to have to be in the same room as Alex over this drive out to Mulga Downs, but can you make sure I'm not left alone with him? I would be so grateful if you could do that."

"Of course, I can. Nothing I enjoy more than playing gooseberry! There were certainly sparks flying between you today. Maybe he's met his match… or have you?" she mused.

Kathy crossed her arms, opening her mouth to retort, and then closed it again, selecting her words more carefully.

"I'm not even playing in this game," she said. "I'm an outsider and always will be."

"Okay," Sarah laughed. "I'll protect you. That what friends are for." She paused, her face screwed in puzzlement. "Are you sure about Melissa? After all, they are neighbours. It is only natural they should get on well."

"Sarah, you told me yourself my first night in town that they were practically a couple. It's obvious he doesn't care for me at all. I was just a mild diversion and that's not a role that suits me."

"Well, from what I've seen, you've disconcerted him as well as diverted him, and for Alex Woodleigh that's really saying something."

Sarah turned to Kathy with a slow smile. "Anyway, what do you feel about him, or is that a silly question?"

There was a telling silence. "He's the rudest, most arrogant, conceited man I've ever met, but... he seems to have this effect on me. I wish I'd never met him!"

"Hey, calm down, kiddo. This is the first man who has ever really got to you, isn't he? I'm not surprised. Not many men would be strong enough. Come to think of it, you wouldn't make such a bad couple."

"Don't be ridiculous! Anyway, it's impossible. Whatever I feel doesn't matter, because what he feels for me isn't very complimentary. If there's anything, it's purely physical. He doesn't care anything for me as a person."

The look she turned on Sarah was beseeching. "Promise me you won't tell anyone. I couldn't bear it if everybody knew."

"What do you take me for? I'm your friend, remember? Don't worry, I shan't tell a soul, and I'll stick close to you next weekend."

"Sarah, you're a dear! We can simply drive out there, pick up Mum and Dad, and turn around and drive right out again. I needn't have anything to do with him at all."

"Don't forget Rose is expecting us for lunch."

"Yes, you're right. How can such a lovely woman have such an obnoxious son? We won't prolong the visit then."

Reflecting she probably shouldn't leave her parents alone any longer, Kathy said goodnight, and made her way back to her own flat. She felt much happier after explaining the situation to Sarah. Not that she had explained a lot as she was so confused within herself.

Why do I let that man get to me? I don't mean anything to him and never will. I should just keep out of his way. Thank goodness Sarah will be there on Sunday.

CHAPTER 9

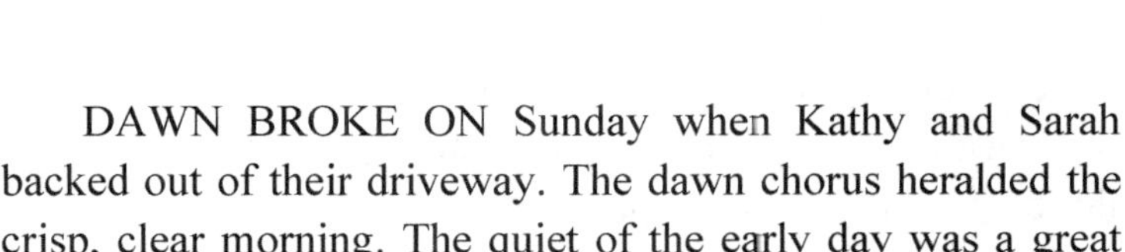

DAWN BROKE ON Sunday when Kathy and Sarah backed out of their driveway. The dawn chorus heralded the crisp, clear morning. The quiet of the early day was a great time in which to travel, with minimal other traffic being another benefit. There wouldn't be much in the direction they were going anyway.

They shared the driving and made good time, even with pulling over in a parking bay for a cup of tea from the thermos they had thought to fill. Once they left the main highway and turned onto the unsealed road leading in the direction of Mulga Downs, their progress was slower. They had to contend with the corrugations in the road surface and the inevitable dust. And the kangaroos. Sarah swerved as a Big Red went bounding across the road in front of the car. She slowed down, commenting, "Where there's one, there's bound to be another."

She was right. A slightly smaller animal followed soon after, a small limb protruding from its front indicating that a joey was in the pouch.

In part they chatted, and in part listened to music, singing along with more enthusiasm than ability. There was something about road trips that brought out the adventurous spirit—not quite Thelma and Louise, but there was still the feeling that one could just keep driving, going wherever the road and inclination took one.

They rumbled over the cattle grid at the gate late morning, and continued the drive to the homestead. The sweeping driveway was edged with agapanthus plants—out of place in this environment but with the ability to survive in low rainfall. Beyond those, was a row of tall Eucalypts with indigenous shrubs filling in the lower storey. Kathy could see they delineated the entrance to the homestead.

Rose had done a good job in challenging circumstances to maintain her garden. Behind an animal-proof fence, they could see a reasonable rose garden and a range of citrus trees, and a series of rainwater tanks. Rose had made a little oasis, with even a vegie patch, with a roof of shade cloth to protect against the fierce sun and then during winter, the biting frosts.

The homestead was typical of the region; a wide-roofed bungalow surrounded on all sides by verandas but enclosed in some parts by louvers and insect screens. A collection of outhouses sat at the rear of the main building. None of the buildings were modern, but looked well-maintained, with the garden growing around the buildings.

Sarah drew up with a toot of the horn, and received a corresponding wave from the group having morning tea on the veranda. An old cattle dog came bounding up to meet them.

162

Even the dogs were happy to see visitors on the station. This one was a sort of canine arbiter for admittance. They had to make the obligatory fuss of the animal before it stepped aside and allowed them to continue up the path. Kathy gave her mother a hug, and Rose a kiss also. On turning to the third person in the group she was confronted by Melissa Gilbert.

"Kathy dear," said Rose "do you know Melissa?"

Kathy turned to the young woman seated on the other side of Rose. As usual, Melissa looked groomed and immaculate, the scarf that was knotted at her throat adding just the right touch—that and the designer label that Kathy was sure it carried.

"Yes—sort of." she said in response to her mother. "Hi Melissa." Melissa's eyes flicked over Kathy and she gave a small nod in her direction with a polite resemblance of a smile.

"You're in time for a cup of tea. Grab a chair from the side veranda and come and join us," invited Rose.

"Sounds great," Sarah enthused. "Washing away the road dust is just what I need. Perhaps we might freshen up first."

"Of course, dear. Kathy, you remember the way don't you? Down the passage and to the right. Use the ensuite off my bedroom." They made their way inside, pausing for a moment for their eyes to adjust from the bright light outside to the dim cool interior of the house.

"What's Melissa doing here?" Sarah hissed.

"I've no idea but she certainly looks at home. I told you there was something going on between her and Alex."

"Hmm. It doesn't necessarily mean anything…" Sarah trailed off. They washed their hands quickly, tidied their hair, and made their way back to the group on the veranda.

Rose had already fetched extra cups. She poured the tea and pushed a plate of biscuits towards the two women. Kathy was hungry—it had been a long time since that early breakfast—but there was no way she was going to scoff biscuits in front of Melissa. The woman sat there looking model-slim and cool, in spite of the rising heat of the day and the irritating little bush flies that were continually in your face.

"Where's Dad?" Kathy asked her mother.

"He's out somewhere with Alex. Not sure what they're doing but he's been having a great time doing it. I've been enjoying the peace and quiet here with Rose."

"And it's been wonderful to have the company," said Rose. "I don't often have the opportunity to socialise with other women out here—except for you of course, Melissa." She patted the young woman's hand. "I love your visits, dear." She turned to Kathy and Sarah. "Melissa was dropped off by her father this morning when he was on his way into town. She joined us for breakfast, so I've been spoilt for company today."

Melissa leant forward and gave Rose an impromptu hug. "You know I love spending time with you Rose. I regard this as a second home really."

Okay, I get the message. Kathy resisted the impulse to roll her eyes.

Her mother and Rose relayed the common interests that they had discovered over the previous couple of days, and Judy described the walk they had taken through a gorge that was not far from the house. She spoke of a beautiful valley, much cooler than the surrounding countryside, and with rock pools at one point providing an important water source for the earlier indigenous inhabitants.

"It's fascinating Kathy," Judy said. "I've learnt such a lot and seen so many new plants. Rose pointed out some of the edible varieties."

Rose must have learnt from the same source as her son. She didn't feel the need to mention the details of her own introduction though.

With morning tea over, Kathy gathered up the cups and tea things and piling them on a tray, carried them inside to the kitchen. Footsteps followed her.

"Sarah, can you get the door? I've got my hands full here."

A well-manicured hand reached past her and held the door open. It belonged to Melissa.

"Oh—thank you." Kathy busied herself with unloading the tray and hoped that Melissa wouldn't hang around. They really had nothing to say to each other.

"I need to go back to Plenty River, and Alex said that you would fly me home. His aircraft is parked in the hangar by the strip."

Kathy regarded the other woman in surprise. She hadn't voiced a request; more of a direction instead.

"Alex said nothing about this to me, and I'm not here for the day you know. As soon as lunch is over, I'm taking my parents back to Alice."

"This won't take long. It's only the next station over. If you leave now, you'll be back in time for lunch—well a little bit late perhaps but it's only a short run by air."

"But didn't you make arrangements for your father to pick you up again on his way past?"

"Father won't be back until this evening. Alex said it would be quicker for you to fly me home."

"Alex needs to speak to me about this himself."

"Well, he can't, can he? He's out somewhere and not contactable for a while. Anyway, I'm only repeating what he said—you could fly me back. I have to be back home by early afternoon and that will be too late for Alex to fly me to Plenty River himself. He's running behind as it is with looking after your parents for the past two days."

Kathy flushed. She was sure her parents hadn't been any trouble but on the other hand perhaps he did want her to save him some time. She hadn't flown Alex's aircraft before but was endorsed on that particular type and model. All the same, each aircraft had its own handling characteristics. "I don't have any charts with me. I wasn't expecting to be doing any flying."

"Alex keeps the local chart in the pocket of the door but you won't need it. It's a clear day and I know the way. It's not as if you'll be going far. The road runs between here and Plenty River anyway. If you are unsure, you can just follow the road." She snorted with amusement.

Kathy realised she had acquiesced without meaning to do so. She wiped her damp hands on the back of her jeans and flicked an annoying strand of hair out of her eyes. Why did she always feel so rumpled in comparison to Melissa? No wonder Alex preferred his elegant neighbour.

"Okay—but we'd better leave now. The sooner we go, the sooner I'm back."

If the others were surprised when Kathy told them what she was doing, they didn't say much.

"Is this far?" queried her mother. "What about your lunch?"

"I won't be long, mum. Save some lunch for me but don't wait before starting. I'll be back soon."

Sarah jumped up. "I'll drive you down to the strip of you like. Do a fly-over of the house on your return and I'll pick you up again."

"Thanks. That would be great. Are you ready, Melissa?"

The three women piled into the car, Melissa in the back. At the hangar, Sarah helped Kathy to push out the aircraft, seizing a moment to ask, "Are you sure about this? It seems unusual to me."

"I was surprised when Melissa approached me," Kathy murmured, "but she says Alex suggested I take her. It must be okay then. Anyway, it means there will be less time that I have to spend with Alex. I'll have a quick bit of lunch on my return and we can head back to town."

"Have you thought this might be Melissa's way of keeping you away from Alex?"

"Oh, that's ridiculous. It's quite clear that I'm no threat to her. I mean, look at her—she has all the looks *and* the neighbouring property as well! A dishevelled pilot who works for her living is no competition."

"Maybe he likes dishevelled. Have you considered that?"

Kathy treated that comment with the disdain it deserved. She did a daily inspection of the aircraft and checked the oil and fuel levels in the tanks. She drained a small amount of fuel and inspected it for water contamination. No problems there. That just left the paperwork. She needed to examine the maintenance release and to record her intended journey. She checked the aircraft. Not there. She looked in the hangar; she couldn't see it there either.

"What's the hold up? We should be on our way by now. We could have been half way there already if you hadn't been fluffing around." Melissa kept looking at her watch.

"I need to find where he keeps the paperwork."

"Oh, we don't bother about that sort of thing out here." Melissa gave a dismissive wave of her hand. "We jump in an aircraft as frequently as we jump in a car. Nobody bothers with formalities for a small flight like this. You'll soon learn—if you stay in the job long enough. If it really worries you, sort it out with Alex when you get back."

Sarah's frown and pursed lips indicated exactly what she was thinking, and it reflected Kathy's level of discomfort.

"Oh, for heaven's sake, let's get going." Turning abruptly, Melissa climbed into the passenger seat of the aircraft. Kathy gave a small sigh.

"Looks like I'm going, Sarah. I'll see you soon. The quicker I am done with this flight the better." She climbed in, secured her seatbelt, turned on the radio. She gave some all-stations calls to advise intentions and the direction of her travel and taxied towards the strip. At the end of the runway, she did her run-up checks, gave a final radio call and commenced her take-off roll.

In spite of the rising heat, the plane climbed smoothly. Kathy trimmed the aircraft at the top of the climb, and took stock of her surroundings. She'd had to bring the seat right forward, and wind it up as far as it could go so that she could see clearly, but she was still conscious of being in Alex's aircraft and sitting in his seat.

They did a circuit of farewell over the homestead and then departed in the direction of Plenty River. In spite of what Melissa had said, there were no charts in the plane. Of course,

Alex didn't need them when he was flying around the property. He knew it all like the back of his hand—and all the routes to the neighbouring properties as well. Charts would have been re-assuring, but Melissa was with her and as had already been said—if all else failed all they needed to do was to follow the road.

"Head in that direction. Aim to the left of that hill on the horizon." Melissa's directions were curt, without extraneous conversation. *Is this part of a strategy to keep me in my place? I feel like a chauffeur.* Still, she followed the directions Melissa indicated. She did after all know the way. Fifty kilometres by road separated the two homesteads, so less as the crow flew. Allowing for a slight headwind one way, and assuming that she didn't hang around at the other end, Kathy estimated that she should be back at Mulga Downs in just over an hour.

She could have filed a flight plan from the air, or at least lodged a Search and Rescue time but, but as it was only a local flight, and Sarah and her parents knew when to expect her back, she didn't bother. She kept a listening watch on the radio but the static and broadcasts picked up indicated nobody else was operating in the region.

She levelled out at four thousand feet above sea level. That left her at around two thousand feet above the ground. It was a great height for observing the landscape below. She wondered if she would spot Alex and her father but she had no idea of the direction they had taken when they left the homestead. She could see cattle in one area—some clustered in the shade of some eucalypts and others around a water trough, but there was no sign of the utility Alex would be driving.

"So—how long have you been in Alice now?"

Kathy was surprised at the question. Melissa hadn't engaged in conversation prior to this, only directions. "A few months."

"You've done well to stick it out this long. It's vastly different to city life up here. Many people stay a short time and then head back to the city and cappuccino territory."

"Well, I'm not one of them. I came up here for the job and I'll stay as long as the position is open to me. I've enjoyed it so far and I've learnt a lot."

"I'm sure you have, but it takes years to understand this country—and the people who live here."

"I suppose so, though I don't think I've had any problem understanding people so far." *Except for Alex and yourself.*

"People are very polite—even to outsiders."

The inference to Kathy that the term outsiders referred to her was blatantly obvious.

"Rose is a dear. I've known her forever. Our families have lived alongside each other for a couple of generations. She's been like a second mother to me. Before long, she will be, in a manner of speaking."

Kathy turned in query to look at her passenger and saw that Melissa was wearing a smug smile.

"There's been an understanding between Alex and myself for some time and it won't be long before we announce our engagement. Alex wanted to give me time to be really sure, and of course I am. I've never doubted this marriage is what I want, nor has he."

The smile now was more possessive. Melissa swept her hair back from her face as she continued.

"Alex flirts with other women of course, but it doesn't mean anything. After all, it's me he loves and that's what's important. I just thought you should know."

"I don't know why you should think it would be of interest to me. I hope you'll be very happy together. I'm sure you're both well suited."

Kathy was tight-lipped, and quietly angry at being warned off. She flushed with annoyance, though her knuckles gripping the control column were white. She busied herself with scanning the instruments, checking that all was as it should be. Anything rather than look at her passenger. The other woman, perhaps sensing that enough had been said, sat back in her seat, and an uneasy silence settled.

The discussion still rankled when some minutes later, the engine began to run roughly. Kathy scanned the instruments, and leaned the mixture slightly to see if that would help. She wished she had greater familiarity with the aircraft. She soon diagnosed the problem. The oil gauge was dropping out of its operating range, and the cylinder head temperature gauge was climbing. What was going on? She had checked the oil before leaving.

"What's happening? Why does it sound like that?" Melissa demanded.

"I don't know. There's a problem with the oil and a couple of the gauges. If they don't stabilize soon, we're in strife."

"I thought you checked everything before we left?"

"I did. There was plenty of oil. I don't understand it!"

"Well do something! Didn't they teach you anything in your training? How could someone so inexperienced have been employed in country like this."

"Be quiet and stop yabbering at me. I need to focus here."

As a first step, she sent out a PAN call on the radio, alerting those within range of the situation on board. She desperately hoped Alex had a radio receiver in the vehicle, and was monitoring local broadcasts.

The silence was deafening. She felt so alone and the presence of Melissa didn't make much difference.

She looked again at the instrument panel. No improvement. The knuckles gripping the control column were still white, but for quite a different reason. She tried to calculate the distance flown and the distance still to travel. Should she turn around and return to Mulga or should she keep going? If she'd been tracking her route on a chart, she would then know exactly where they were. If only she hadn't agreed to Melissa's demands. If only…

The trend in each gauge was becoming marked. Unless she put down somewhere fast, they would be in real trouble. If the engine seized, she would lose control, and Alex wouldn't thank her for damaging the engine—permanently. She had to land when she could select the location and control the rate of descent. She needed to make a forced landing and to shut down the engine… fast!

"It's no good. I'll have to put down somewhere. Do you know of any bush strips in range?"

"Not before we reach Plenty River. Can't we keep going until then?"

"No, we can't. The sooner we're on the ground, the better. We need a safe landing spot. Keep an eye out on your side for a clearing."

Kathy worked at maintaining their height while they both frantically scanned the country below. It looked hopeless. The ground was densely vegetated, further compromised by creeks and rocky outcrops. A landing wasn't possible. If they'd followed the road, they could have landed on that but following Melissa's instructions they had headed cross country.

Kathy reviewed the instrument panel. The oil gauge was in the red and they were losing height. The engine was now exceedingly rough and noisy. They had to shout to make themselves heard. She had practised plenty of forced landing exercises during her training, but none of them had quite prepared her for this. Their chances of surviving unscathed, or even alive were decreasing by the minute. Why, oh why, hadn't she climbed higher in the first place? At least then she would have had more height to play with.

"We're running out of options." Kathy screamed the instructions, not daring to look away from the vista below. "We're going down anyway, but I'll try to aim between the trees. That way the cabin might stay intact, even if the wings are ripped off. Make sure your harness is tight. Secure any loose items. Open your door now so that it doesn't get jammed shut on landing. There could be a fire after we get down, so get out quickly and run like hell."

As Melissa frantically stowed the loose items, Kathy sent out a Mayday call, repeating the call sign of the aircraft and advising her intentions. There was no discernible acknowledgement—only static. Did Alex have an emergency beacon in this aircraft? He must have, but she hadn't thought to check. She opened her door as well, with the slipstream holding it in place.

"Melissa, I've got to focus on getting us down. You keep trying the radio."

There was no response. Wasn't anybody listening? Melissa flicked through some other radio frequencies, still with no success. Probably more height was needed to bring them into range. That was something they didn't have.

There was even less height to play with now. Kathy watched the altimeter winding down steadily. A band of fear tightened around her chest. How had she put them in this situation? How would they get out of it? She eased back on the throttle and applied a stage of flap. She needed to set the aircraft up in the best possible landing configuration.

Suddenly, she spotted a small clearing ahead. It didn't offer much room, but what other choice did she have? They were going down anyway.

The trees before the clearing were a problem. Her only hope was to skim over the top and then drop down quickly. She had done short field landings before, but that was when the aircraft was fully operational and she could apply full power and go around if she wasn't happy with her approach. Not this time. She muttered to herself, her knees starting to tremble as she directionally controlled the aircraft with the rudder pedals. "Keep calm, girl, keep calm," she kept repeating. "Any landing you walk away from is a good one." The throw-away line at pilot barbecues had seemed a joke— until now.

The ground rose to meet them. "Brace!" Kathy screamed, completing the emergency checks, and then switching the electrical system off. After a moment's hesitation, she switched the fuel selector to OFF also. She was committed to landing, and could glide in if the engine cut out before she was on the ground.

They were so close to the tree tops that Kathy expected to hear or feel the foliage brushing through the undercarriage. She fought to retain height, but still needed to keep the nose down to keep the aircraft above stalling speed. The clearing was in front of them and she cut the last of the power. There was little fuel left in the lines anyway and the engine was already spluttering. They dropped to the ground, or else the ground rose up. The aircraft bounced heavily. Fighting to maintain control, Kathy forced the nose back down, and braked as hard as she could. She had to stop before she reached the scrub at the end of the clearing. Her mouth was dry and her jaw ached from clenching her teeth. Her knees shuddered. She could vaguely hear Melissa screaming beside her but her world had become a small bubble of intense effort. Everything was happening so quickly. They were going to plough into some dense undergrowth soon and before reaching that, the ground was rocky and uneven – more so than it had looked from the air. She hauled on the hand brake to help slow them down.

There was a sickening thud and a tearing of metal. A wheel collapsed as the aircraft slewed violently and spun around. With a gasp of alarm, Kathy pitched sideways and cracked her head on the side of the cabin.

Then there was silence.

CHAPTER 10

ALEX AND BOB pulled up at the homestead just on twelve thirty, with the inevitable cloud of dust billowing behind. The dog went through the same meet-and-greet routine, and was rewarded with attention from Bob who obligingly rubbed the dog's head and scratched him behind the ears. This only served to make the welcome even more exuberant than before.

"Down, Rusty. Get down!" Cattle dogs were working dogs and Alex didn't usually make a big fuss of them, fond as he was of the old red kelpie. "We'd better get inside and washed up. Mum's sure to have lunch on the table by now and she doesn't like to be kept waiting."

"That's understandable. No arguments from me. It's been a long time since breakfast. I see the girls are here." Bob nodded in the direction of Sarah's car, now parked in the shade of a stringy bark tree. "They must be inside with Rose and Judy."

The two men walked around to the back door. Here they removed their work boots before stepping inside, the screen door shutting with a resounding slap behind them. They entered the mud room, where Alex hung up his hat and jacket before they both washed up in the hand basin. They made themselves presentable before joining the women in the dining room.

Lunch was laid out, with food covers in place to ensure that none of those sticky flies got to the food before the diners did. There were greetings all round and Judy of course got a hug from Bob. He looked around and spied Sarah, and she got a hug too. He had grown fond of the young woman in the short time he'd known her.

"Mum," said Alex, "did you get a call from Tim Hinkler, the mechanic from Central Avionics?"

"No dear. Should I have?"

"I left a message for him to call. I'll check the office phone. Won't be long. I'll be back in two ticks."

He turned and headed out of the room, leaving the others chatting about their morning. They were all seated and helping themselves to the cold meats and salads when Alex re-joined them.

"There was a message. Tim must have rung while you were all outside. He has to be out this way on Tuesday so he'll drop in then. I didn't want to wait that long, but I guess I've got no choice."

"Why? What's the matter?" Rose inquired.

"Didn't I tell you? The oil pressure is playing up on the Cessna and I need Tim to check it out." He spooned a generous portion of potato salad onto his plate. "I love your salad Mum, it's the best." He didn't immediately notice the silence in the room.

"Where's Kathy?" Bob asked. "She's usually the first to be in for lunch. Don't know where that girl stacks it all."

"Kathy flew Melissa back to Plenty River," explained Sarah. Her voice was strained.

"She'd better hurry or there'll be nothing left. I'm famished!"

"I don't understand," said Rose. "Alex, if there was a problem with the aircraft, why did you tell Kathy to fly Melissa home?"

Alex paused, fork in mid-air. "I didn't tell Kathy anything. I haven't even seen her. What are you talking about?"

"Melissa said you left a message," Sarah explained. "She said you told her to tell Kathy she needed to fly Melissa back to Plenty River. Melissa said she had to get home and you'd said it would be helpful if Kathy flew her."

"Are you saying they've taken the Cessna?" His voice rose in disbelief.

"Well, yes. Kathy wasn't comfortable with it, particularly as she couldn't find the maintenance release, but Melissa was insistent this was what you'd instructed, and that you never bothered with paperwork out here anyway," said Sarah

"What utter rubbish. Of course, I do. The maintenance release is here in the office. I brought it inside with me when I rang and left a message for Tim. There is no way I would have left those instructions for Kathy." He looked as incredulous as he sounded. "Bloody hell. I wouldn't have flown the aircraft myself, let alone asked anyone else to. What on earth was Melissa thinking?"

"I don't understand," said Rose. "Why would Melissa say Alex had asked for Kathy to fly her back, when clearly, he hadn't? She's usually such a sensible young woman."

Sarah chose her words carefully. "Kathy's a good pilot. You know she's not a risk taker. I'm sure they'll both be fine."

Alex pushed his chair back from the table. "I'd better go and ring Plenty River and check they've arrived. If Kathy is there, she'd better not fly back again. What a mess!" This last comment was flung over his shoulder as he strode out of the dining room, leaving a disconcerted group behind him. Nobody was eating, not even Bob.

"Blast." Alex slammed the phone down. His call to Plenty River confirmed that the aircraft had not arrived, and there was no sign of it. While he had waited on the line, the station manager at Plenty had gone outside and scanned the sky. When he came back, the news was not encouraging.

"Not a sign, mate. All quiet. I'll rustle up a couple of the men and we'll head out in the direction of your place. Do you know the route they will have taken?"

"No idea. I wasn't aware they were planning this little trip. Melissa has some explaining to do!"

"Okay—all we can do is head along the road in case we can spot anything. We'll have the radios with us. Give us a call if you learn anything further."

"Will do. Thanks for your help. I'll get on to Flight Service and see if they've heard anything. If they've made a forced landing, Kathy should have been able to send out a call first."

He scrambled frantically through paperwork looking for the right phone number, until remembering he usually kept it in a directory near the phone. "Come on," he muttered, "pick up the phone! What are you guys doing in there?"

"Alice Springs Flight Service." The voice at the other end was brisk.

"G'day. It's Alex Woodleigh here. Our aircraft is overdue at Plenty River and I wondered if you'd had any broadcasts logged. Call sign Romeo Juliet Quebec."

"Roger that, Alex. John Robinson here. A Mayday call was logged at 11:35 local time this morning. Static was bad and most of the broadcast was undecipherable. We heard a female voice but couldn't pick up the call sign. We're going over the recording at the moment trying to identify more detail."

Alex felt the blood drain from his face. The news was not good. What would he tell Kathy's parents—and Dan Gilbert for that matter? He listened intently to what John Robinson was saying.

We do know the pilot was making an emergency landing, but don't know where or how many people were on board. Since that call no further communication has been received and nobody has picked up an emergency beacon as yet. An emergency phase has been declared. What can you tell us, mate?"

Alex explained the circumstances as best he knew them, giving an indication of the route they would most likely have followed, based on his usual flight path to Plenty River. He also told them a ground party was leaving Plenty River to do a search as best they could.

"Roger, Alex. Standby—I'll just relay what you've told me and we'll scramble the search and rescue team. Back shortly." The line went quiet while the Flight Service Officer made his report. Alex could faintly hear voices in the background as he paced the office in agitation.

"Alex—are you there?"

"Yes."

"We're swinging into action. We're contacting StationAir and two aircraft are re-fuelling now and heading out to Mulga Downs. The search and rescue will be coordinated from there. Have someone contactable at all times. We'll keep in touch. Gotta go mate. Things to do. We're still calling the aircraft in case someone can hear us. Talk to you soon." With that, he was gone.

Alex sat in silence, his thoughts in a whirl. Without an aircraft he felt so helpless! If only he'd left the maintenance release in the hangar or at least told his mother about the problem, he knew Kathy would never have taken off. He should have said something. He couldn't forgive himself if anything had happened to her. Never in a million years did he think that Melissa would pull a stunt like this. What was so important she had to get back home? She'd said nothing about it earlier!

As he re-entered the dining room, Alex was aware of four pair of eyes turned in his direction.

"And?" queried Sarah.

"Look, I don't want to alarm you too much. They've made a forced landing somewhere. When I heard that they hadn't turned up at Plenty, I rang Flight Service and was told a mayday call had been received. Reception was bad, so they don't know where exactly, but a search and rescue team is on its way out from Alice. They'll come here first and I'll brief them on the route Kathy will most likely have taken. They'll set up a search pattern after that."

Bob took Judy in his arms, his wife starting to tear up. "Judy love, our girl will be okay. She's sensible is our Kathy. She'll have put down somewhere—perhaps on the road and is sitting out there now waiting for someone to come and get her. We'll find them in no time."

"I'm so sorry." Alex was anguished. "If only I'd told mum about the oil pressure, this would never have happened. I was so focused on doing that bore run this morning that I clean forgot about it."

"Alex, it's not your fault. With Judy and I being here, we've probably thrown your routine out of wack. We don't blame you. Anyway, our girl's going to be fine."

Bob's voice sounded confident. Alex could only wish he felt the same.

Rose stood up. "Sarah dear, can you put the kettle on and make a pot of tea? You'll find everything you need in the kitchen. At this point I think we all need a cuppa."

Sarah jumped up, pleased to have something useful to do.

"I'm going to contact Tom Daly at Jinka Station," Rose said. "I was listening to the morning chat session and heard that Chris and Mark are doing some mustering work over there today. They're much closer than Alice. If we get onto them, they should be here soon." She crossed to the radio receiver.

"Jinka, come in please. This is Mulga Downs. Over."

"Go ahead Rose. What's up? Over"

She quickly filled them in. Fortunately, Mark and Chris were at the homestead for lunch. When they heard what Rose had to say, they were out the door and running for their machines before the call was finished.

"Mum, if they've got enough fuel to get to Mulga, they can refuel once they're here," Alex called.

"It's all right. I've already told them that. They're on their way. Now Alex, sit down and have some lunch and have a cup of tea. It will be a while before the boys are here and you need to have something to eat before you go out again."

"I can't sit down, Mum. I'll get the charts and work out the track for the search aircraft. I feel useless just waiting here. I've got to be doing something."

"I'll put together some sandwiches," said Judy. "I know what you mean—I've got to do something too. I'll include some for those chopper boys. If they've run out without their lunch, they'll be hungry. Rose, can we make up a thermos?"

Mark and Chris arrived a short time later, to the relief of all concerned. While they re-fuelled, Alex briefed them on what had happened and where he thought the women were most likely to be. These were mustering choppers, so not able to take more than one passenger each. They decided that Mark would fly the route of the road to Plenty, and Bob would follow the same route in the 4WD. Alex and Chris would take the more direct route that he normally flew, on the assumption this was probably the way Melissa would have directed Kathy.

Rose manned the station radio, and Sarah was briefed on their planned course of action so she could advise the search crew who were on their way out from Alice. She would be monitoring the HF frequency which all the aircraft would be using.

Chris, Mark and Alex climbed into the machines, donned headphones and gave a brief nod to the anxious party left behind. With an all stations broadcast on the HF local radio frequency, the choppers rose into the air, nosed onto their selected tracks and departed, Mark in one direction and Chris and Alex in the other. A dust trail already indicated Bob's departure route.

Climbing to sufficient height to give them good visibility on either side of their track, Chris and Alex scanned the ground. They kept in constant contact with Mark over the radio, and could also hear the periodic calls being made from Alice Springs in an attempt to make contact with the stricken aircraft. Chris tried as well in the hope that perhaps reception would be better in their close vicinity.

"Romeo Juliet Quebec, this is helicopter Mike Tango Bravo. Do you read?" Shortly after, they heard Mark send a duplicate call.

There was no answer to either of them. Their sense of foreboding grew with each unacknowledged broadcast. Alex knew that when the search team arrived from Alice, a grid pattern would be established and each aircraft would have to fly a specific segment to be sure the country was well covered between Mulga and Plenty. In the meantime, he was hoping that by flying the direct route, they would find the aircraft quickly without having to resort to the broader and more systematic search.

"Mike Tango Delta, this is Mike Tango Bravo. Change to company frequency." Chris and Mark both selected their company frequency on the radio. They were free to chat without observing aeronautical protocols and without clogging up the airways. "Mark, any sightings?" Chris asked.

"Negative. I can see the cloud of dust behind Bob's vehicle, but nothing else. Some cattle and a couple of roos a few minutes ago but no sign of the aircraft."

"All okay, Mark. Nothing here either. Some of the bush coming up is quite dense. I might reduce height to get a better view through the canopy."

"Copied that. Keep yourself safe buddy."

"Sure, you too. Over and out." Chris selected the official channel again in time for him and Alex to hear another call to the missing aircraft from Flight Service.

There was still no reply.

"What's that over there?" Chris pushed forward slightly on the stick so they could both see what he was talking about and then swung around to give Alex an uninterrupted view from his side window. "It looks like a section of fuselage."

"What? It can't be!" Alex peered intently, then gave a sigh of relief. "It's clear you don't fly fixed wing mate. That is an old fuel drum. Been there for years. Doesn't look like any part of a fuselage!"

"Okay, okay – I only got a glimpse of it anyway. Happy it's not."

"How 'bout you do the flying and leave the spotting to me." Alex didn't mean to sound so terse, but when Chris had mentioned a section of a fuselage, his heart had jumped.

Chris was aware of his agitation. "Don't jump to too many conclusions. It's early days. I'm sure Kathy and your fiancé will be fine."

"Fiancé?" queried Alex. "We're not engaged. What gave you that idea?"

"Sorry—my mistake. Girlfriend then. I'm sure we'll find your girlfriend safe and sound."

Alex sounded exasperated. "I don't know where you get your information from but she's not my girlfriend either."

"Okay—I just thought from the local grapevine there was an understanding in place. My mistake."

"You mean Melissa?" Alex's voice rose a notch. "Melissa's like a sister to me. We grew up together, but there's nothing more to it than that."

"Yeah right," Chris muttered softly. "Have you told Melissa all of this?"

The bush became denser on the ground beneath them and the foliage and canopy obscured sight of anything beneath. Alex realised if they weren't flying directly over the aircraft, they wouldn't see it at all.

"What was the wind direction late morning?" he asked Chris. "If they drifted off track, where might they be?"

"Look, the search and rescue team will have those calculations done. Best we just stick to the track and then we know where we've been. A successful search has got to be systematic. At least I can't see any smoke on the horizon."

"Smoke! I don't even want to think about that! Look if they're hurt in any way, the sooner we find them, the better. What was that wind direction? We won't stray far off track— just a little in the direction of possible drift."

Chris acquiesced, and Alex did a few calculations on the back of an old flight plan that was in the chopper. "Okay—as far as we know, she didn't access any weather reports and was flying with visual reference so wouldn't have compensated in calculating the track to fly. She may have drifted slightly to the left, though not far over this distance. Still, we should keep our eyes peeled to that side as well."

Chris grunted in response. He picked up the microphone again. "Romeo Juliet Quebec do you read? Romeo Juliet Quebec come in please." There was no answer from the missing aircraft but the radio crackled into life.

"Mike Tango Delta this is Alice Springs. Can you give an update please?"

Chris responded. "Alice Springs, current location adjacent Whygo Well. No contact established with the aircraft. We'll keep trying."

Mark came online as well confirming his location and unsuccessful attempts at attempting contact. They kept the detail brief. Others could be monitoring the frequency as well.

As Alex scanned the ground below, he saw a section of tree top that looked to have been damaged. Could it have been caused by an aircraft crashing through the canopy? He tapped Chris on the arm and indicated that he should fly in that direction to check it out. Chris nodded in assent and spiralled lower in order to see clearly from every angle. They could see a branch had broken off, but peering intently, couldn't see any sign of the aircraft on the ground. It might have just been one of those times when the tree dropped a limb, perhaps in response to heat stress.

Satisfied finally there was nothing else to see, Alex gave Chris the nod and the chopper climbed again and Chris guided the machine back onto their previous track. They flew in silence for a while, having exhausted conversation.

Suddenly, Alex got a glimpse of something white. "This way! Look—there might be something over there!" The two men stared as Chris swung the chopper around, and tracked in the direction Alex indicated, and carefully maintaining height.

"If there's something to see, I'll drop down for a closer look. It's not likely though. If they'd come down here, we'd see some tree damage."

Alex was glued to the window. "There it is!" He grabbed Chris's arm. "Over here. Swing around this way. See it?"

There on the ground was the aircraft. It slumped at an awkward angle at the edge of a small clearing but seemed to be in one piece. There was no movement that they could see.

"My God!" exclaimed Alex. "How did she manage to put down there? She must have literally dropped it into that space." *Kathy, please be all right! Where are you?*

Chris picked up the microphone. He needed to advise the aircraft sighting ASAP. "Alice Springs this is Helicopter Mike Tango Delta. We have the aircraft sighted on the ground. No sign of movement but we're about to make a landing to investigate further."

"Roger that Mike Tango Bravo. We'll await further advice."

The Chopper swung over the clearing and hovered, preparing for descent. They could see the aircraft clearly now. When they were only a couple of hundred feet off the ground, a figure emerged from under a tree, waving frantically.

"Look—there's someone. They must be all right." Chris chose his landing place carefully, taking note of the wind direction from the movement of the surrounding trees.

"I can't see so clearly—yes it's… no… it's Melissa." Alex had his face pressed against the windscreen as he peered down. The chopper barely settled on the ground before he released the seatbelt and threw open the door. Keeping low to avoid the spinning rotors, he ran towards the woman.

Melissa ran forward to meet him. She was dishevelled and her face was tear-stained but other than that she seemed to be all right.

"Alex, thank goodness you came. I've been so scared." Sobbing, she threw herself into his arms. "I'm sorry, I'm so sorry."

"Don't worry about that now—are you hurt? Are you all right?"

"I'm bruised from the seat belt and probably some whiplash but otherwise I think I'm fine." She sniffed, and a wet patch was left on Alex's shirt. Sure now that Melissa was mostly severely shaken up, Alex gave her a quick hug and a pat on the back, then unwound her arms from around his neck. Pushing her away, he ran to the aircraft. The cabin was empty.

"Kathy! Where's Kathy?"

"I got her out," Melissa whimpered, unable to miss the concern in his voice. "She was worried about a fire on impact, so I dragged her out. I thought she was dead at first. I put her in the shade over here."

Turning in the direction Melissa was pointing, he could see a figure lying under the tree. He hurried over, closely followed by Chris who by this time had fully shut down the chopper. Kathy lay limply, blood oozing from a nasty gash on the side of her head. Looking at the stains down the front of her shirt, it had bled copiously.

"Ooh—nasty," muttered Chris. "I'll get the first aid kit. Lucky I always carry one with me." He hurried back with the kit and a bottle of water as well to find Alex brushing the matted hair away from Kathy's face.

"Okay mate. If you move aside, I'll just get her patched up. First Aid qualifications are a compulsory part of our job."

He turned back to Alex, who was hovering at this shoulder.

"If you want to make yourself useful, get on the radio and let everybody know they're going to be all right. I reckon there are a few people waiting on that information. Tell them also we'll need a medical evacuation. They can pick her up from Mulga. We'll get her back there."

Chris was right. He needed to make that call.

Alex hurried over to the chopper and set about switching the electrics and the radio back on and made the broadcast. Fortunately, there was still coverage on the ground. He put a call through to Rose on the frequency used by the local properties, so she could assure everyone that although Kathy was injured, it didn't look to be life-threatening.

"Thank goodness" The relief in Rose's voice was palpable. "I'll make sure Plenty River Station heard the news. They'll be so worried about Melissa. "I'll let Bob know he can turn around and come home as well."

As Alex hurried back to the others, he could see Chris had opened up his medical kit and was organizing the water and swabs.

"Kathy, can you hear me? It's Chris here, sweetheart. You've got yourself a bump on the head, but I'm going to clean you up, and then we'll see about getting you out of here. I reckon you'll have a headache for a while."

There was no response. Alex hoped her injuries weren't more serious than they'd first thought. Donning a pair of sterile gloves, Chris washed away some of the blood and then secured absorbent wadding to her wound, with a length of bandage wound around her head.

As he worked, Melissa explained what had happened. She glossed over taking the aircraft without permission and her role in persuading Kathy this was what Alex had directed. She explained the mechanical problem that developed and the fact Kathy said they had no choice but to make a controlled landing while they still had a choice.

"I've never been so scared—I thought we had no chance of survival," she whispered, choked with emotion again as she relived the experience. "I thought we'd had it. We came down hard and fast, and bounced a couple of times while Kathy tried to pull up and then we hit this huge rock hidden in the grass. She couldn't have avoided it if she'd tried. The wheel was torn off and that's when it happened."

She was hiccupping through her tears and the two men had to listen intently to understand what she was saying.

"I thought she was dead; I thought I'd killed her." Another paroxysm of sobbing followed. Alex was amazed that Melissa had managed to manoeuvre Kathy out of the plane and to drag her into the shade. They could see the drag marks in the grass left by Kathy's heels.

Soft moans and a whimper alerted them to the fact Kathy was slowly becoming more alert. Her eyelids fluttered before shutting again.

"Hurt… my head…" Her voice dissolved into a whimper again.

"Kathy you're safe. Everything is going to be fine. We'll have you lifted out of here in no time." Alex held her hand, not daring to touch her head again.

A whumping sound above alerted them to Mark's impending arrival. He put down at the far edge of the clearing, so the dust and debris stirred up barely reached them. The whump turned into a whine of decreasing volume as the rotors slowed. They were all pleased to see him, just knowing there was more support on the ground.

The issue of getting them all out of there was discussed. Each helicopter could only take one passenger besides the pilot, so Alex suggested that Chris take Melissa home to Plenty River Station, and on the way back to Mulga, stop off at the crash site and pick up Alex. He could also pick up more fuel at Plenty River. Helicopters used for mustering never had much of a range, and the last thing he wanted was to run dry. In the meantime, Mark could take Kathy back to Mulga Downs.

Kathy was not up to walking, so Alex scooped her up in his arms, and picked his way carefully through the grass and stones to Mike Tango Bravo. Mark climbed in from his side and they both made sure that the seatbelt was secure, before Mark gave the thumbs up and indicated to everyone to stand clear. They stood and watched as the chopper rose, and then disappeared beyond the trees.

"Climb aboard Melissa and we'll be on our way. The tom toms have reached Plenty River and I reckon everyone will be anxious to see you too." Chris directed her towards his machine and climbed in on his side, donning his headphones and turning on the avionics. Melissa hesitated, turning back towards Alex.

"Alex, you know I never meant any of this to happen, don't you?" She lifted her tear-stained face to look into his eyes. "I always thought… my father wanted… it's her, isn't it?" She stumbled over the words. "I've sensed something each time I've seen you together."

"Melissa, you mean a lot to me. You were there when Dave died and you've been a big support to Mum over the years. You know I've always loved you and always will, but I love you like the sister you've always been."

Her tears started to well again. She stared at him wordlessly, her anguish visible before abruptly turning and running towards the waiting chopper. Climbing aboard and strapping herself in, she refused to look in his direction. As the machine lifted in the air, he was aware however of her white face, quite unreadable, staring down at him. The helicopter rotated onto the required flight path and was gone. Alex was left alone.

After the two machines and their passengers had gone, Alex surveyed the sad state of his aircraft. How in the hell was he going to get it out of there? It would be both difficult and expensive. He walked around it to assess the results of the impact. He was relieved to see the damage was not huge, but qualified investigations would be required to assess that. It would have to be air-lifted out of that location. It couldn't be repaired in situ and it could never be flown out. He'd worry about the mechanics of that later.

He went and sat back down in the shade of the same tree that had provided shelter for the two women. With little else to do he reflected on the unexpected feelings for Kathy. He'd not only admitted them to others today, but also to himself. Like it or not, she was under his skin and he didn't know what he was going to do about it.

CHAPTER 11

PETE HAD RUNG of course. It hadn't taken long for the grapevine to tell him of the events. He spoke to Kathy's parents first as they had answered the phone at the apartment and they had given him an outline of what happened. They had assured Pete he could ring Kathy in hospital. They were sure she would welcome his call. He was one of the last people to whom she'd wanted to speak.

"Hi Kathy, sweetheart. How are you feeling? It's Pete here."

"Yes, I recognised your voice. I'm fine thanks."

"I hope you're on your way to recovery. You gave everyone such a fright--your parents, myself and or course everyone from Skyways."

Oh no. *Did you really have to discuss it with all of them? That is too embarrassing to even think about.* As if things weren't bad enough already. Aloud she said, "Thank everybody for their concern, but I expect to be out of hospital and back at work soon."

"Look, I know you were enjoying Alice and your job and you're working with a really great people, but don't you think it would be better if you found employment back here? I can put feelers out for you if you'd like," Pete offered.

"Short answer—no. There is no way I'm running away from Alice with my tail between my legs." This wasn't a conversation she wanted to have. "Look, I have a headache. I'm sorry but I'll have to go."

Terminating the call, Kathy knew she'd been abrupt but how dare Pete suggest she should leave town? She wasn't going to give up on either her job or her dream. She was still steaming when Sarah dropped in with the latest news. Kathy was so relieved to see a supportive face.

"What are people saying, Sarah? Are they blaming me for what happened? Do you think my future prospects here are over when they've hardly begun?"

"Don't be silly—of course not. Do you have something I can put these flowers in? Everyone from the office sends their regards by the way. Here's a get-well card—everyone signed it."

"That's lovely. Thank them for me."

She looked earnestly at Sarah, trying to control the emotion that threatened to over-spill.

"Pete just rang. He was trying to persuade me to go back to a safe job in Adelaide. I don't want to do that; it would feel so much like giving up, but do you think that's what I ought to do? Am I out of my depth here?

"Don't listen to what Pete has to say. You know he has his own agenda. You stick to yours. You may have a bit to learn yet, but this is a great place to get that experience. Don't give up on us now. I've just got used to having you around!"

Impulsively, Sarah gave her friend a hug.

"I know you feel bad about what happened, but don't forget—I was there too. I heard what Melissa had to say, and she lied! She deliberately lied. She was the one who put your lives in danger. I'll back you up all the way."

"Sarah, I'm so pleased you're my friend, but who else will believe me over what Melissa has to say? She's part of the establishment around here. People will take her word before mine."

"Actually…" Sarah paused, considering Kathy pensively and twisting one of the stray curls that always seemed to decorate her face. "…I don't know what has prompted it but Melissa has sort of come clean. She's admitted Alex didn't ask you to take the aircraft, and also admitted she told you Alex never filled in the maintenance release. I've just heard this second hand, but you know what the grapevine is like around here. It's so astonishing I reckon it must be true. That will surely go in your favour."

Kathy had been both surprised and confused. "She wasn't too friendly towards me in the air—that much I do remember. She was very particular about warning me off her precious Alex. I had the feeling she wouldn't give me a drink of water if I was stranded in the desert in the middle of summer. I wonder what brought on this change of heart?"

"I've no idea. Anyway, my lunch time is about over. I'd better get back to the office before someone starts asking questions. I'll pop in again tomorrow if you're still here. Otherwise, I'll see you at home."

Kathy had been relieved at the conversation with Sarah. It had settled her mind but she was still ruminating on the issues, seated in the chair by the window when a soft knock on the door of her room announced another visitor. Alex stood there holding an enormous bunch of flowers, beautiful Lisianthus blooms in creamy whites and purples.

"Alex! What are you doing here?"

"I would have thought that was obvious. Visiting you. How are you feeling?"

Kathy pulled her dressing gown closer around her, feeling exposed and at a disadvantage as he stood over her. "I'm fine thanks. Much better. Should be out of here soon."

There was a pause and he'd looked around awkwardly, clearly not sure what to do with the flowers.

"I brought you some flowers."

"Yes, I can see. Thank you, they're lovely."

She chewed her lip. How did he know they were her favourites? What was he doing here anyway, with or without flowers? Perhaps Rose asked him to bring them and Alex was just the courier.

"Umm … if you put them in the sink, I'll ask the nurse shortly to get me a vase or a jar or something."

He looked uncomfortable, which was very strange for Alex. Perhaps hospitals were out of his comfort zone. He was probably working out how to start tearing strips off her. There was another silence and then both started to speak.

"Alex, I'm so sorry…"

"Kathy, I just wanted to say…"

They each stopped, looking expectantly at the other.

Gosh, this is excruciating, but I need to get this out. As she opened her mouth to start again, the door opened and her doctor bustled in on his rounds.

"How's my patient feeling today? I see you're out of bed. That's good. I'll just check a few things. How are you sleeping?" He picked up her medical notes from the metal pocket at the end of her bed.

"Look, I'll catch you later Kathy. I'll give you and Doc some privacy." With that Alex was gone, leaving her flushed and flustered.

"Your boyfriend needn't have rushed off," said the doctor distractedly as he absorbed her notes. "I won't be long here. I'm happy with your progress so I think you're ready to go home in the morning. Take things easy for a while and keep your ribs strapped up. I'll need to see you back in a week to take the stitches out and I'll check the wound then as well."

Boyfriend? Whatever gave him that idea? Aloud she'd said, "Thank you. I'll be pleased to sleep in my own bed again." The dreams she'd been having in hospital were disturbing, replaying events from the accident again.

"Don't forget to pick up the x-ray films from the ward desk on your way out. You'll need those later for your medical review. I'll write a cover letter as well on your progress and will get someone to drop it in to you before you leave. Now remember, any problems—headaches, blurred vision, anything, come straight back in here. I'll give you a sick certificate for the rest of the month. Is there someone to keep an eye on you at home?"

She'd already had a barrage of tests to ensure that there were no consequences that were not immediately obvious. Kathy knew she would be required to undergo additional testing from an aviation medical examiner before she could return to work. Head injuries were regarded with concern and she would need that clearance before Rob Collins would let her back in an aircraft.

With assurances she had noted his instructions and that yes indeed there was someone to keep an eye on her, the doctor slid his pen back into his top pocket, and continued on his way, leaving Kathy with her thoughts and her bunch of Lisianthus.

Feeling strangely flat and deflated as well as incredibly sore every time she drew breath, Kathy allowed herself to be guided to where Gordon was parked. She'd only remained in hospital a couple of days, but the whole experience had left her feeling weak and teary.

She'd learned the details of the crash landing and subsequent search and rescue from Sarah and was embarrassed at the drama she had caused. On top of that, a journalist had come in seeking details and she'd had to make a police report as well. Her parents visited daily as had a steady stream of other visitors, but she was still mortified at what had happened. She shouldn't have listened to Melissa. She shouldn't have flown that aircraft.

As the pilot, it had been her responsibility not to take off without seeing the maintenance release. She should have sought confirmation from Alex that she had permission to fly the aircraft. Quite simply, she should have known better. An incident like this would stain her record for ever, and of course there would be an air safety investigation into the circumstances of the incident. Just thinking of that was enough to leave her flushed and agitated.

Part of her didn't want to leave the hospital. If she stayed there, she could delay having to confront the consequences, whatever they may be. The other part wanted to be home and in her own space. She was fortunate to have her own room but even so, hospital routines and general activity were not conducive to peaceful rest. Also, she didn't think she would have quite as many visitors at home and although she was grateful for everyone's concern, and all the wonderful flowers that she had received, she wasn't feeling her most social.

Sarah had lent the car to Bob and Judy for the day so they could pick Kathy up from the hospital. They were still staying at the flat, and Kathy admitted to relief in coming home to the ministrations of her mother. She didn't feel up to looking after herself. She felt guilty though at having spoilt their holiday and said as much to her mother.

"Don't worry about it, dear. We've managed to extend our visit. There was no way we were going home and leaving you in recovery mode. We've been able to juggle any commitments at home so you're stuck with us for a little longer—if you don't mind, that is."

"Mum, of course I don't mind. It's not much of a holiday for you, that's all."

"Well, we had that lovely visit with Rose, and people have been most kind to us while you've been in hospital."

Her father pulled up at the front door of the flat, and Kathy gingerly eased herself out of the car. As her mother opened the front door, she could see the flat was a mass of flowers. There were some from work, with a message from Rob Collins that under no circumstances was she to come back until she was one hundred per cent fit. She'd only brought the one bouquet home from the hospital. The rest she had left in the ward to be distributed to any patients who didn't have any, but she couldn't bear to leave the beautiful Lisianthus behind.

On the drive home, they'd stopped briefly at a homewares store and Judy had slipped in and purchased a lovely glass vase. As she said, they had exhausted all the jam jars in the unit complex. The only other alternative was a bucket and that was not considered an acceptable solution.

"It's so good to be home," Kathy said. "I might have a cup of tea and then lie down for a while though. I'm more tired than I expected."

Lying on her bed, she still puzzled over the visit Alex had paid her in hospital. What had he been going to say? He must be so annoyed but he hadn't come across that way at all. It really didn't matter. She had a dreadful headache, and was too tired to think. The greater problem was, what on earth would *she* to say to him about his aeroplane? To bend your own plane was poor form, if you were fortunate enough to have one, but to bend someone else's was unforgivable.

She spent the rest of the afternoon going through her mail, sorting out some bills which needed to be paid, and working briefly on her account of the forced landing and everything leading up to it. She knew she would be called upon to provide a written statement, and probably more than once. She needed the time to sort out the sequence of events in her mind.

Everybody dropped in after work of course, with Chris and Mark carrying on as usual and filling her in on some of the details of the search.

"That was some landing Kathy," said Mark. "If you're going to keep trying to get into tight spaces like that, I reckon you should take up flying choppers. They might be more your style!"

"Go away you two." Sarah was stern with them, though nobody was fooled. "I'm not sure that you set any sort of example for Kathy to follow. Look at you both now, tiring her out."

"I'm fine," Kathy lied. In truth her head was still troubling her. "I really want to thank you both. I don't remember it all, but I've been told you led the advance party looking for me and I really appreciate all you did."

"Aw shucks," said Chris. "It was nothing, especially for a pretty lady like you."

She had to laugh but still, she was glad when they all went home. She'd had enough for one day. After picking at a light dinner, Kathy retired early. She still felt woozy. The hospital had given her some sedatives to help her sleep if necessary, but she preferred to do without. Instead, she had a restless night, tossing and turning and finally drifting into a sleep that was plagued with re-runs of the accident.

Again, she experienced the agonising knowledge of what was about to happen, felt her sweaty palms, the surge of adrenalin as the ground rushed up to meet her, and the dreadful crunching noise as the aircraft came to grief. Inexplicably, Alex was there too. Why was that? He hadn't been in the aircraft. He seemed to be holding her and stroking her face, all the while talking softly to her. Why wasn't he berating her?

"Kathy love, I'm here. I've got you now."

The dream disintegrated into a mixture of helicopters and aeroplanes, and Kathy woke with a whimper to find her mother sitting by the bed, patting her hand gently.

"Kathy love, I'm here," Judy said. "You're all right now—it was just a bad dream."

"Oh mum, it was so real, all over again. I keep having different versions of the same dream, all focused on the accident. I'm going through that landing over and over again."

"Flip your pillow over—it will be cool on the other side—and I'll make you a warm mug of milk. That will help you get back to sleep."

"That would be wonderful. It's just what you used to do when I was little."

"I did, didn't I, and it'll help you now just as it did then."

Gratefully sipping the warm milk, Kathy relayed what she could remember of the dream.

"I thought someone was patting my hand. Different scenarios keep playing out in my dreams. I must be processing such a lot. I hope it stops soon.

She glanced at her mother.

"Melissa wasn't patting my hand, that's for sure, though I'm grateful to her for looking after me. I've been told she dragged me out of the aircraft and put me under the tree. The consequences if there'd been a fire just don't bear thinking about."

Judy smiled sympathetically. "I think you'll be fine to go back to sleep now Kathy. And as for that young woman," she added. "So she should have looked after you. Her antics put you in that situation in the first place. She could have killed you both." Her disapproval of Melissa was apparent. "I'll leave the hall light on in case you have another dream but I don't think you will. Good night love."

The next day, reassured by Kathy's protests that she would be perfectly all right, her parents went for a walk. The pantry needed replenishing, and it gave them a good excuse for a leisurely stroll whilst making their purchases.

"I'll be fine—honestly. Looking at the galleries is a great idea. Don't forget the Arunta Gallery in Hartley Street. It has some wonderful paintings on display. If you want to have lunch at one of the cafés in town, I'll fend for myself. There's plenty of food here, so you needn't rush back."

"Well, I'm pleased to see you looking so much better Kathy." Bob kissed his daughter on the cheek. "We'll see you later then. You could probably do with some time on your own anyway."

Feeling a sham, for she was really much better, Kathy settled on the veranda in the filtered sunlight with a book, and a cool drink beside her. Before long she would be bored and would be rattling her cage for something to do but right now, doing nothing very much was just what the doctor ordered. With the warmth on her face, and the merest hint of a breeze, she settled back with her feet up on another chair, and closed her eyes.

Muzzily through her doze, she heard footsteps. They were back quicker than she expected. But there was only one pair. Opening her eyes, Kathy was startled and dismayed to find Alex standing over her.

"So, you're home then?"

"Yes."

"We didn't get time for much of a chat at the hospital, so I thought I'd drop in here instead. You don't mind?"

"No, of course not. I understand there are a few things that we need to discuss."

Inwardly she was panicking. She knew that this conversation was inevitable, but hadn't expected to have it today.

"Umm – would you like a drink? I have some iced tea."

"That would suit me too. Don't get up – I can help myself. I assume it's in the fridge?"

"Yes. Glasses are in a cupboard to the right."

He ambled inside with an assurance that surprised her. When he returned, he brought the jug with him.

"I thought you might like a top up." He filled his glass and refilled Kathy's. While he was occupied, she took the opportunity of observing him without it being so obvious. There was an authority and confidence to his actions. He didn't give the impression of someone who ever experienced self-doubt.

She removed her feet from the other chair so he could sit down. He pulled it up within easy reach of the cane table on which the jug and glasses rested.

Alex nodded in the direction of the flat. "I see you've got a few flowers in there."

"Yes a few. I've been spoilt. Please thank Rose for me by the way."

"Sure, but what for in particular?"

"Well for the Lisianthus. Mum must have told her how much I love them. She's so thoughtful."

"You're sort of right. Your dad who told me. So, how's the head feeling?"

"Better, thank you. I think it's made of tough stuff. Takes more than a bump on the cranium to put me out of action. The ribs are still sore. I have to be careful how I move." She took a sip of tea as she garnered some strength. She wasn't quite sure where to start this conversation.

"Alex, I want to apologise. What I did in taking your aircraft was inexcusable, and even more so to break it like I did. I should have known you would have a maintenance release somewhere and I should have looked for it." She glanced at him quickly, then looked away before continuing. He had a look on his face she couldn't decipher. "I know the damage will be quite costly and it will take me a long time to do it but I'll compensate you every cent for the cost of the repairs. It is repairable, isn't it?"

"Kathy… will you just be quiet and listen?! That's not what I came to talk about. Firstly, I'm more concerned with your health than the condition of the plane." The tone of voice was more like the Alex she knew, but she now regarded him with some puzzlement.

"As you can see, I am well on the way to recovery." She paused, and this time looked directly at him. "You must be very relieved Melissa wasn't hurt beyond shock and a few bruises."

"Melissa…" he said shortly, "I've sorted a few things out with her. In fact, we've had rather a long chat. Sometimes you just let things drift along, but the events of recent days made me realize I've been a fool. When the chance of happiness comes your way, then you need to seize it."

"Oh absolutely," Kathy agreed, hoping she didn't sound quite as pathetic as she felt. At least some good must have arisen from the accident.

He continued as though she hadn't spoken. "We had a brief chat at the crash site after you and Mark took off, but I realised afterwards that I didn't handle it as well as I could have. I made the time to talk with her yesterday. I think we've now come to an understanding."

Suddenly, the sun seemed unbearably hot, and Kathy had an urge to get away—to lie down alone in the cool darkness of her room. Anywhere rather than here in a one-on-one situation with Alex while he talked about his future plans.

"Let me be the first to congratulate you," she said stiffly. "I hope you'll both be very happy."

"Both be happy? What do you mean? I'm not going to marry Melissa! Isn't that what I have just been telling you? That's what I've cleared the air about. I'm very fond of Liss, of course, and always will be. She was there for me in a dark time of my life and I'll always be grateful for that."

He sat forward in his chair, looking at her beseechingly.

"Once you get to know her, she's a great person—really funny and a loyal mate. We more or less grew up together you know. She's like a sister to me." His eyes never left Kathy's as he paused to take a mouthful of his tea.

"Melissa deserves someone who'll make her really happy, and I know that person could never be me. Ultimately, she would want a different lifestyle to the one I could offer her."

"Umm yes… I'm sure you're right." Kathy was unsure how to respond to this conversation. The description of Melissa as funny and a great mate was difficult to take in. Why was he telling her all this? "So, if you don't want to talk about the plane—and we still have to do that at some time—what do you want to talk to me about?"

"Well first, I just wanted to see how you were, and to be sure that you were on the road to recovery. Then, I thought seeing as you're off work for a while, you might like to join me for a picnic lunch—if you feel up to it."

"Picnic!" This, she did not expect. The prospect of a picnic with Alex Woodleigh was not something she had considered, nor spending convivial time with him. Where did he have in mind? Some local waterhole perhaps? The memories which arose at the thought brought a flush to her cheeks.

"Okay—perhaps ants and flies aren't a good idea just yet. We might skip the picnic today." He paused, observing her. "Grab your shoes and hat anyway. There's somewhere else I'd like to go instead."

"But why should I go anywhere with you? Where exactly are you planning on taking me?" Kathy was unsure of what was being proposed here.

"Well, to answer the first question, because I'm such a nice person, because… it's a great day to do something different, because… you're only going to sit home if you don't go. As for the second question—to the sale yards."

"Sale yards—selling what?"

He looked at her in some surprise. "Cattle of course. You're in cattle country, you know. We can stop by the café on the Stuart Highway and pick up one of their steak sandwiches. They're compulsory when you attend the sales. Not that I'm buying anything today—nor selling either for that matter, but I want to keep track of the prices that are being achieved. There are also a couple of people I need to speak to. It's a good place to do that."

"Look, I don't think you want me tagging along after you at the sale yards. I don't know anything about cattle, expect basically one end from the other." Kathy was bemused and a little confused by the suggestion.

"I thought you said that you wanted to learn more about the industry."

"Yes, I did, but…"

"Well now is your chance. If you were serious that is.

"All right, all right… I'm coming." Kathy glared at him. "Give me a couple of minutes."

What is he playing at? It's such an odd suggestion. She grabbed her hat and a water bottle and headed back outside after leaving a note for her parents. Alex leaned against the side of the Land Cruiser, waiting for her. On her approach, he straightened and opened the passenger door and offered her his arm to ensure she didn't have any difficulty climbing inside. Even this courtesy unsettled her. He was not behaving to pattern at all.

Not many spaces remained in the parking lot by the café, with the lunchtime crowd jostling for places. Alex ordered two steak sandwiches with the lot, and they retreated to a bench under a tree outside to eat them. As he said, eating these creations was a dedicated task, and not to be considered while driving or dealing with other distractions.

Dealing with the dribbles trickling down her forearms, Kathy had to agree. She was used to a wafer-thin piece of meat that hid amongst the shredded lettuce and was slid between two nondescript pieces of bread. This was real steak, with egg and onions and slices of beetroot and tomato and shredded lettuce and probably other things if she cared to investigate. The bread was sliced from a huge doorstop loaf, and from the taste and texture, was oven-baked sour dough.

"That was absolutely de-lish," Kathy said as she fed crusts to some waiting magpies. "I can't eat any more but I understand why this place is so popular. I haven't been here before." She was tempted to lick her fingers as well, but resorted to the paper serviettes instead.

"There's probably a lot that you haven't done in Alice. Consider today part of your education." Alex cleared up the detritus from their meal and put it in the bin. "We need to get going."

When they arrived at the sale yards, the auctions were in full swing. The auctioneer moved from pen to pen, with a swarm of buyers, sellers and stock agents following behind. Kathy could hardly make sense of the sales patter over the noise. It entailed a whole new language which everyone else could understand and not her.

Alex wanted to introduce a new stud bull to Mulga Downs and was investigating the merits of a particular beast he had his eye on. There were various people with whom he was able to discuss the characteristics he was looking for and the potential changes he would make to the herds. The animal was likely to be offered the following week.

It was kind of interesting and she absorbed all sorts of cattle-related information, but by mid-afternoon, Kathy began to wilt. She had a looming headache, and knew she had been on her feet long enough. She quietly sought out a bench in the shade, leaving Alex to his comparisons and discussions. The unusual afternoon left her with a lot to contemplate.

"Kathy, I'm sorry." Alex came hurrying over. "You look done-in. Why didn't you say something? I'd better get you home."

She made a polite protest, but was secretly happy when he escorted her back to the car. A chance to have a rest would be welcome and she was pleased when they pulled up in the driveway. Bob and Judy were on the veranda having an afternoon coffee, but Alex declined her invitation to come in.

"You need a rest. You don't want me hanging around. Say hello to your parents for me."

"Yes okay—but Alex, we still need to talk about your aeroplane."

"I guess we do, but now is not the time. I have to stay in town for a couple of days, so I can pop in tomorrow. I have a few things to do early morning, so say about 11:30? Will that suit?"

"Yes of course. I don't have any other plans at the moment. Just taking it easy really."

"Good. I hope your lesson in cattle management was not too overwhelming? I thought if you're going to hang around the Centre for a while, you might like to acquire some industry knowledge." He had a quirky tone to his voice, and Kathy looked at him quizzically, but his bland expression gave nothing away.

She opened the car door. "It was very interesting—thank you. Not what I was expecting from today but then life is full of surprises. I'll see you tomorrow".

Before she could get out, Alex leant across and lightly kissed her on the cheek. "Tomorrow," he agreed. She was so startled that she slipped out of the car without any further response, and watched him drive off. Who was this man? Certainly not the Alex she knew.

If her parents thought anything was unusual about her day's outing, nothing was said. Nor did they comment when she said Alex was coming around the following day, although as Kathy explained, there was still some discussion to be had about the plane.

"I'm sure that you'll get it sorted out between you," Bob said. "Alex strikes me as a very reasonable man. I liked what I saw of him during our stay on the station. He's extended an open invitation for us to come again."

Oh, has he now. It's like Alice in Wonderland—curiouser and curiouser. Not that she minded. *Not at all.*

CHAPTER 12

THOUGHT OF THE discussion to come left Kathy a nervous wreck, and it showed. She examined her bank account to review her savings and calculated how much she could save from her salary on an ongoing basis—except she didn't quite know what the damage bill would be.

Her parents could do little to reassure her, except to repeat again they thought Alex was very reasonable and surely some agreement would be reached.

"You don't know him like I do," retorted Kathy. "Don't let that man fool you. He's as nice as pie around other people or his mother, but there's another side to him as well and it's not admirable."

"Whatever do you mean, Kathy?" inquired Judy.

"Just take my word for it Mum. I don't want to go into specifics now, but suffice to say he doesn't really have a lot of time for people from the city. He's rather intolerant."

"Oh well, I'm sure you know what you're talking about."

There was nothing further to be gained from the conversation, and Kathy retreated to her chair on the veranda, making an unsuccessful attempt to lose herself in her book. Her parents had copies of the local newspaper and also settled themselves on the veranda. Alex finally drew up in the driveway at about 11:35. Such was Kathy's mounting anxiety, that she felt slightly nauseous and less than welcoming. In fact, as he walked towards her, she pointedly studied her watch.

She looked up to see the jeans of the previous day and been swapped for moleskins, and the mid-blue of his cambric shirt enhanced the colour of his eyes. Kathy absorbed all this in a moment. He looked good but she was determined not to acknowledge it. Why did the sight of him make her pulse quicken? There was no point to that. She steeled herself for the discussion she knew would follow.

"Okay," he called as he approached. "I know I'm running slightly late, but it's not that bad, is it?" He nodded to her parents. "Bob, Judy… good to see you."

"Morning Alex. Bob and I are just about to fold the washing, aren't we Bob, and then we need to make a cup of tea," Judy said

With a roll of his eyes, Bob followed Judy into the flat, but not before giving Alex a discreet wink. Not so discreet that Kathy didn't see it with some annoyance.

"Well," said Alex to Kathy. "Good morning to you too. You're obviously overjoyed to see me."

"Look, I don't mean to be rude, but I really need to get this aeroplane business sorted. I've been trying to work out my finances and think that…"

"That's great news Kathy but I'm not sure this is the best place to have that type of discussion. We might find somewhere a little more private."

"Like where, for instance? What did you have in mind?" She was cautious about being in a non-public place with him, although she felt more than capable of handling anything that he might try.

"Don't worry. I'm not planning anything dastardly. All above board and not too tiring, I promise."

"I'm quite all right now. You don't have to worry about me getting tired or anything like that."

That was a lie, but she wasn't going to admit to any weakness in front of him.

"Good. Tell your parents we'll be back after lunch and we'll be off."

"You haven't said where we're going?"

"No, I haven't, have I?" He grinned. "Sometimes you just have to put your trust in other people. I promise I won't take you any place where no one will hear you scream, but it will be quiet enough for us to talk undisturbed."

Not wanting to sound any more churlish than she already did, Kathy quickly told Bob and Judy that they were going out, climbed carefully into the front of the Land Cruiser and buckled up around her tender ribs. Why all the secrecy? She didn't understand.

She didn't have to wonder for long. Alex drove to the top of Anzac Hill. She hadn't expected him to take her there.

"This has always been one of my favourite thinking places, if I'm in town that is. Surprisingly, not many people come up here unless for Anzac Day or similar commemorations. It's really peaceful and besides the fantastic view, the solid presence of this great lump of dirt and granite is sort of comforting.

He parked the car, and moved around to the passenger side to open her door, hovering in case she needed help in getting out. They walked over to the edge of the lookout.

"From here, I can see the span of the MacDonnell Ranges, and that's reassuring too. They're sort of like sentries – ancient guardians of this place. Perhaps it's the clear air, but I seem to make better decisions up here. I thought it might be conducive to our discussions."

He removed a large basket from the back of the vehicle. "Mum packed a picnic lunch for us and there's something cold to drink as well."

"Rose… is she in town?"

"Yeah. I think she's been in frequent contact with your parents and asked me to bring her with me when I said that I was driving back into Alice. They may be planning a catch-up of their own. She'd like to see you too. She probably wants to see for herself that you're OK.

"Hmm," Kathy said. "My parents seem to have been spreading themselves around. Rose has been good to them. I'd like to catch up with her as well."

Alex laughed. "I've long since learnt that my mother has a way of organizing people and events to her satisfaction. She gets on well with your mother, so the contact probably suits them both."

Like mother like son? Kathy kept that thought to herself.

Alex looked around him, basket still in hand. "There aren't many flies or ants up here at this time of day, so I thought we'd be safe with the pseudo picnic. There's even a table and bench so we can set up in style and you don't have to sit on the ground."

He placed the basket on the table, leaving Kathy with no choice but to follow. The light breeze playing on top of the hill ruffled her hair, sending the wispy blond tendrils on a dance. She had lost a little weight over the past week, but was regaining her appetite. She was intrigued to see what Rose had supplied. As she helped him to unpack the basket, Kathy reflected on the irony of the location Alex had chosen, and the reasons behind it as well. Perhaps they had more in common than she had thought.

"Sarah introduced me to this spot on my first day in town and it's been special to me ever since. There's something magical about the view, particularly at sunrise and sunset."

"Ah yes, the delightful Sarah. I felt so sorry for her—she and Dave made a great couple. That's another thing—I've always felt closer to Dave up here." He sighed. "She's right about the magical times, but for today, midday is going to have to do. Drink?"

He set the glasses on the table and poured two glasses of chilled wine. A selection of gourmet sandwiches followed, with some cheeses and fresh fruit. Even a couple of foil-wrapped chocolates. *At least he picnics in style.* She took her drink and a strawberry for good measure.

"Thanks, but Alex, we need to have this discussion. I really need to get the details on the table."

"Do you realize that's the first time you've used my name?"

"Not until you mentioned it. Is that important?"

"At least you are acknowledging me as a person and that *is* a change."

"Don't be ridiculous. Of course, you're a person."

"Yes, but one you've been holding at arms' length, and I rather wish you wouldn't."

"I don't know what you're talking about. Anyway, didn't we come up here to talk about the repairs? Like I've already told you, I fully intend to make good the damage; it just might take me a little time. Considering the circumstances behind the flight, you're probably not covered by insurance and so this will be an out-of-pocket expense for you. Do you have any idea what the repair bill will be? It is repairable, isn't it?"

"Of course, it is. The wheel and strut will have to be replaced but luckily there was no propeller damage and the fuselage seems to be fine as well. It all needs to be checked over by the mechanic– there may be some minor bits and pieces that need replacing but I think it will be okay. I have a new wheel on order already. Might be here in a couple of days."

"That's much better than I'd hoped. You must let me know how much I owe you. I'll repay you as soon as I can. I'll be back at work soon and I don't have a lot of other expenses."

Alex leant across the table, and gently stroked the side of her face.

"I can think of some rather creative ways that you can repay me," he murmured.

Kathy stared. "What do you mean? Are you expecting me to work off this debt on my back?" The pain of her indignation seared her chest. She pushed his hand away and leapt up from the table, surveying him angrily, hands on hips.

"I don't believe you just said that. How could you think such a thing?"

"Kathy—damn, I've botched this terribly."

"You sure have. You've totally misunderstood me, but then you've done that from day one, haven't you?" Now she was angry. Really angry.

"Kathy listen; it's not what you think. Sit down again, please."

"I've heard enough."

"Just hear me out. That's all I ask—for now anyway. Sit down while I try to explain."

Gingerly, she sat at the table again. She reached for her wine but made sure to keep out of hand's reach.

He continued. "What did you think of our little excursion yesterday to the sale yards?"

She was puzzled by his change of tack. "Umm—dusty and noisy and confusing at times, but I picked up some of the jargon and what the buyers were looking for and the sellers were hoping for. What has that got to do with anything?"

He was silent for a moment, as though trying to work out what to say next. "I wanted you to see what lies beneath the surface of this town, to understand some of the industry that sustains it. I wanted to know if this is something in which you might develop more of an interest… if you could live with the cattle and the dust and the flies and all that goes with it.

"What are you suggesting? That I visit Mulga Downs sometimes?"

"I'm not talking about visiting for a weekend here and there; I am talking about a lifestyle—a whole new life in fact."

"You mean work with cattle? Is that what you're saying? You expect me to be some sort of Jillaroo?" She threw back her head and laughed. "I think you've got rocks in your head."

"No, I meant *living* with cattle, not *working* with cattle, though the two go hand-in-hand to an extent. Could you see yourself living on a station, dealing with the remoteness and to some extent the isolation—not on your own of course but with a partner who cares deeply for you and your welfare?"

Her heart quickened. She was not sure that she really understood the direction of this conversation and she so very much didn't want to get it wrong.

"It's not something I've thought about before" she said hesitantly. "I've concentrated on my flying career. There hasn't been any reason to do otherwise." Her eyes rose to meet his, and after a brief pause, he continued.

"Kathy, how do I get you to understand me— it's you that I want. God help me, I never thought that I would fall for a girl from the city. It takes a lot to understand a life on the land. Even your father asked if I knew what I was doing, and said I'd be taking on a handful. He wasn't exactly telling me anything that I didn't already know."

"My father? What do you mean? Have you and my father been discussing me behind my back! If you've got anything to say to me, say it to my face, not to my father. It's nothing to do with him." She spluttered with indignation. "I've heard enough. I think you'd better take me home."

"It wasn't like that. God woman, you go off quicker than a Chinese cracker on New Year's Eve. Are you always like this? Your father and I didn't set out to discuss you by any means. I saw him down at the hospital the other day—you were asleep at the time—and we just got talking. I don't suppose he told you I was there."

He pushed his fingers through his hair, leaving it looking tousled and slightly appealing. The nervous response action gave him an oddly boyish look.

"I told your father what Melissa had done, fabricating the whole thing about me asking you to fly her back to Plenty River. Then the fact that I had taken the maintenance release out of the plane and how dreadfully sorry I was about everything that happened.

He ran his fingers through his hair again, before turning an earnest look on her.

"The last thing in the world I wanted was for any harm to come to you, or for your father to think I'd put you in danger. We just got talking that's all. He's a good bloke. We got on quite well over the couple of days he and Judy spent with us."

Kathy glared at him, wishing she had smashed his aeroplane into little tiny pieces. Where did she fit into these cozy little chats—while she was sleeping, no less? And why hadn't her father told her about this visit?

"Kathy, you look priceless when you're so angry. You know, the day when we stop arguing is the day that we're going to be in trouble!"

"We? There is no *we*."

"We don't have to rush into things just yet, but here in the bush we're long-term strategists, and when we know we're onto a sure thing we act on it. I've learnt how to size up a heifer and I've always admired your feisty spirit."

"So now you are calling me a cow. See—I did pick up some terms at the sale yards. Is that how you see me? You really know how to make a girl feel good about herself. I can't wait for the encore."

"Kathy, it's not as if I'm not talking about putting a brand on you, but don't you think there's the possibility of a future together?"

She didn't answer him. She couldn't. She was so floored she had absolutely no idea what to say. Her heart thudded loudly enough for Alex to hear. This conversation was incredibly confusing.

He continued. "I know some people have made assumptions about me and Melissa, but that's all they were—assumptions. I've been quite uncommitted—until now that is. What I'm trying to say is you're not like any other woman I've met before. You're gutsy, and argumentative, and obstinate, and irritating, and determined – and you've got totally under my skin!"

"You could have fooled me. If this is how you demonstrate attraction, I'd hate to see your response to someone you truly didn't like."

"Kathy, you talk too much, and rubbish at that!" He grinned and pulled her close to him. "I think I've done enough talking for a while. Perhaps you can understand this."

Drawing her closer still, he kissed her tenderly. Her reaction was instinctive. She wasn't ready for this. She placed her hands against his chest, bracing herself and ready to push away. The trouble was, there was that small inner voice that said she didn't want to. She relaxed a little, her fingers fanning out against him and no longer tensed. His response was to draw her closer, his lips becoming more demanding.

Her head spun and she couldn't blame it on the accident. With renewed strength, she pushed them apart.

"You can't…"

"Shut up and kiss me you fool."

This time, she complied. *I must be still concussed. None of this is really happening, and if that's the case, I might as well make the most of it.*

She surprised herself in realizing she enjoyed it. She wanted more. Her body had a mind of its own as she melted into him, moaning softly. *If this is still part of my dream, don't stop.* Her fingers began to trace a path of their own down his chest, gently exploring and teasing.

"What are you doing to me, Kathy? Actually, I know what you're doing and I like it!"

She gasped as now he began a series of little nibbles, trailing from the side of her mouth and down her neck and she arched against him in pleasure, eyes closed.

"Mm… and I get the feeling you like it too."

The sound of a car pulling into the car park penetrated her senses. Her eyes sprang open. *What's happening here? This is absolutely crazy. This is a man who has treated me abysmally!* She pulled away, dishevelled and with bruised lips.

"But you hurt me. Your behaviour after that day at the waterhole emotionally shattered me. I gave myself totally to you and then you acted as though I didn't exist."

"Kathy, believe me, that was never my intention. I was a thoughtless bastard but you totally knocked me for six. My head was all over the place, and I took it out on you. I wanted to talk to you later, but when I looked around you were gone."

"Is that surprising? Not only did you ignore me when we returned to Arapunya, but you allowed Melissa Gilbert to wrap herself around you. The messages I received from both of you were loud and clear."

Kathy dropped her eyes from his and wrapped her arms around herself, gripping her elbows in a protective gesture.

Alex seized her by the upper arms, forcing her to look up at him again.

"I need you to know that the events of that day were spontaneous. I didn't plan it and I don't regret it either; not a moment of it. You've been in my thoughts since then; before that really. I remember you from the very first time I saw you, a bewildered-looking woman standing beside the Ghan."

"You're kidding—you glared at me!"

"True, but you made an impression on me even then, and you've been doing so ever since."

"You made an impression on me too, but for all the wrong reasons," Kathy retorted.

"Well, I do feel guilty about that. I was probably out of line your first day in flight briefing."

"Probably! More like definitely." There was a hint of scorn in her voice. "I wasn't expecting quite such anachronistic attitudes."

"Ouch. It's no excuse, but Dave Bishop was a childhood friend of mine. We grew up together, went away to boarding school, got up to all sorts of trouble in our teenage years. He was the sort of mate I knew I could always depend on. Then he went and got sick and ended up dying. That wasn't in the script at all. I was angry at him for dying and then I was angry at you for trying to take his place."

Kathy struggled to hide her exasperation. When she spoke again, it was in a slower and more measured tone, though not unsympathetic.

"I'm sorry about Dave. I was told about him shortly after I started with StationAir but I didn't know you were so close. I understand how much you must have missed him, but at that point, I didn't even know he existed. I could never take his place, but StationAir needed a new pilot and I needed a job. Was that really such a problem?"

224

"No, it wasn't—only in my head. It was just a shock really. It's wrong to say I'm over it because that almost suggests that I'm 'over' Dave, but I'm dealing with his loss in a healthier way. I think, right now I might have Dave's seal of approval."

"Is that so? You think that Dave would approve of a city girl, taking over his job and his friends?"

Alex laughed. "I'm sure he would, given who it is." Grasping her shoulders, he held her at arms' length, his steely grey eyes gazing directly into hers. "And what's your impression of me now? Has it been formed for all the right reasons? Does that impression encompass a future together?"

"Future together? You think I've come up here just to find a husband. You don't take me or my job seriously. How can we have a future together?"

"I'm not talking about rushing into anything. For now, it's enough you know what I feel for you." He nibbled her ear again. "We can wait a little while." He held her at arms' length again so he could study her response. "I think you've done a marvellous job of finding a potential husband, seeing as you found me. I know what flying means to you. You're not such a bad pilot, even though you bent my aeroplane, and I'm sure we can come to some advantageous arrangement whereby you can pay me back."

He kissed her on the tip of her nose, laughing at her squirming response.

"You could still keep flying for StationAir, but there is a lot of flying to be done on the station as well you know. I'll expect you out at Mulga Downs at every opportunity to work off some of that debt."

Kathy stared at him, trying to process what she was hearing. Did he really say he had feelings for her? Was he playing with her emotions? She could hardly admit her feelings to herself, let alone to him.

"Well? Aren't you going to say anything? Do you think you could consider a future with me?"

"A future! If you're talking marriage, I'm not ready to take that step."

"Kathy, just stop teasing, and playing with semantics. I want us to have a future together because I love you, you enticing woman. Who else can land an aircraft in a tight spot like you? I'll ask you the question now if it makes a difference. Will you marry me?"

He got down on his knees before her and struck a beseeching pose. He looked so ridiculous, she burst into laughter.

"Get up! Ask me again later and I might consider it. I need time to process all of this. On the other hand, what other man do I know who owns an aeroplane?

CHAPTER 13

COMPLYING WITH THE check flight requirements was nerve-wracking. There were two in fact. The first was to be completed with an examiner from the Department of Aviation, after she had passed her medical examination. The second was with Rob Collins.

"I have no doubts about your ability, Kathy," he said, "but we have to satisfy our insurers. You'll feel better in yourself as well if you know you've ticked all the boxes."

The look he gave her was wry.

"I know how certain events can really undermine your confidence. This will reassure you that you still have the required skills and competencies."

Kathy wondered what events in Rob's past might have prompted these comments but knew better than to ask. If he wanted her to know any more, he would tell her.

The check flights were scheduled for the same day. Having them over and done with in a relatively short time frame made sense, but also meant a full day of pressure and anxiety.

Bob and Judy had already returned to Adelaide, so she had the flat to herself. The evening before, she ironed her uniform and checked the contents of her backpack. She had reviewed the handling notes for the aircraft, but left them out on the dining table in case she needed to look at them again. Then she checked the backpack once more.

"Relax," Sarah advised when they caught up briefly after dinner. "If you were totally blasé about this, I might be concerned but you'll be fine. It's just your professionalism that's making you nervous. You set yourself such high standards."

"Sure—me, and the Department, and Rob Collins, and the local community, the odd passenger—anyone else I've left out?"

"You'll be fine." Changing the subject, she asked, "Have you decided whether or not you'll attend your friend's wedding?"

"I'd like to. Mum and Dad brought the invitation with them when they visited. Jessie was my closest friend at school. I'd love to be there for her. She's the first of my friends to walk down the aisle. I'm hesitant to put in a leave request right now though."

"You're entitled to it. You would have some accrued leave. Speak to Rob about it after your test."

Kathy was getting ready for bed and still considering the question of the wedding when the phone rang. She knew who it would be.

"I know it's late, but I wanted to wish you luck for tomorrow." The voice was encouraging.

"So, you think I'll need it, Alex?" she teased.

There was an exasperated sigh. "Sweetheart, you know as well as I do, you'll ace it. I thought you might like the moral support that's all. And to hear from me of course."

"I am grateful. I must have driven Sarah crazy with my anxiety, so it's probably reasonable to give her a break and transfer the angst to someone else."

"Anytime, sweetheart. I'll always have a listening ear. I should see you on the weekend so you can tell me about it in person then."

In spite of her teasing, she appreciated the call. It indicated a considerate side to the man, one which a few weeks ago, she would not have anticipated. Climbing into bed, she was surprised to realise her anxiety was easing. She knew her skills hadn't vaporised. Tomorrow was just a formality.

The scene in the aircraft hangar was an indication that some things never changed. As usual, the radio was playing and although everyone was busy, there was a fair amount of chat thrown around across aircraft cowlings.

"Kathy! Good to see you back. What are you up to today? Planning on stacking any more planes?" Colin bounced up to her with a cheeky grin, making it plain that she needn't think she was excused from future teasing.

"Leave her alone, Col. It's the girl's first day back," admonished one of the others. "Like to see you attempt a landing like that. You'd just bend over and kiss your arse goodbye!"

There was reassurance in the consistency. The examiner from the Department was already in the company office. He wandered out and watched as she performed the daily inspection on the aircraft she was to fly. After advising her passenger she was ready, they both strapped themselves in and Kathy taxied towards the holding point.

It wasn't by the book, but in responding to her initial radio call, the ground controller acknowledged her personally.

"Roger Alpha Sierra Victor, area QNH is one zero zero niner, cleared for take-off. Welcome back, Kathy."

The examiner threw her a quick glance, eyebrows raised. "Seems you have a local cheer squad."

"You know how it is in a small town," she responded. "Everyone knows everything about everyone else."

She noted his small smile of acknowledgement, before lining up on the centre line and applying full throttle. The heat of the day had not yet set in and there was no discernible turbulence. Applying steady back pressure to the control column, she felt the aircraft lift and they were off the ground. She was in control once more.

Sarah and Alex had been right. Once she was airborne, she was back in her element. She relaxed into the tasks and confidently performed all the manoeuvres that were asked of her. She even enjoyed it. She'd missed it. She was competent and it showed. There was a slight hiccup when she lost height on a steep turn, but on her second attempt, the procedure was perfect. Even so, as they joined the circuit area for her final landing sequence, she was aware that her tension had lifted. Switching on the cabin fan and directing the flow to her face, she was confident she was ready to return to work.

The men in the hangar watched her taxi in and park on the apron area. Kathy and the examiner exited the aircraft and walked towards the StationAir office. The silence from the hangar was unnatural. Kathy gave a surreptitious thumbs-up and was rewarded with a grin from Colin and a corresponding gesture. They had all been rooting for her.

She was far more relaxed for the subsequent flight with Rob Collins. Although he was more important to her on a personal level, Kathy knew it would be difficult for him to find fault with her when a Department Examiner had found her to be competent and cleared to fly again.

"You haven't lost your touch, Kathy. You'll do." Rob wasn't a man of many words, but a nod from him was worth a few. They had tied down the aircraft and were walking back into the airport office.

"Thanks Boss. So, I'm back on the roster?"

"If you feel you're ready. Everyone will be pleased to see you. Enquiries on your wellbeing are a daily occurrence in the office at the moment."

"Sarah has told me. I've been touched by everyone's concern. It has really made me feel a part of this community." She paused, looking at him uncertainly. "There's something I need to ask you."

"Oh? And what's that?"

"An old friend in Adelaide is getting married in six weeks' time and I've been invited to the wedding. I know I've just had time off, but can I take leave for a week to attend the wedding and sort out a couple of issues back home?"

"I don't see any problem with that. You're entitled to the leave after all. Submit your dates and the leave application form and we'll manage the roster from there. Speak to Sarah about the arrangements."

As she said to Sarah later, she was relieved on all counts.

"Now I can think more constructively about my future."

"You weren't seriously worried, were you? Or do you have other issues on your mind? You wouldn't hold back on important gossip? I won't tell a soul—promise!"

Sarah had this way of sniffing out information she considered vital to her knowledge of the world. She now stood up from her chair and came around to the front of her desk, where Kathy was hovering.

"Does this have some bearing on what's happening with you and Alex?"

Kathy rolled her eyes. "Has anyone mentioned you have an over-active imagination?"

"Lots of people—many times." She sighed theatrically. "This I what I'm reduced to—living vicariously through the exciting lives of others."

Kathy felt a fleeting stab of guilt. How unfair was it that life was on the upturn for her, yet nothing was changed for Sarah?

"I'm sorry, Sarah. I was full of myself and what's happening in my life. I didn't mean to be so insensitive."

"Listen to me. You are not being insensitive. I don't expect the world to stop turning because of my situation. What happened was far worse for Dave than for me. I'm just happy for you. Promise you won't make me wear an ugly bridesmaid dress!"

"Now your imagination is really running away with you. For now, we're being civil with each other. That's a big step, surely?"

"Okay—so he was being civil all night on Thursday, was he?"

"Is nothing private in this town?" Kathy laughed in exasperation. "Silly question. Don't bother answering. Of course, it's not." She paused.

"Anyway, I've got more important things to consider—like what will I wear to this wedding in Adelaide. I might undertake some research."

It wasn't an official workday for her, although the company was paying for her time during the testing process. Otherwise, she was free. She strolled down Todd Mall, browsing the shop windows and considering her options. Tourists and locals alike meandered down the Mall, avoiding the sun and sticking to the shade of either the verandas or the street trees. As she contemplated which café might be the best place for a coffee, a voice hailed her from behind.

"Young Kathy. Fancy running into you."

She turned around. Tom Daly strode along the footpath and looked delighted to see her. His hat was still firmly fixed to his head, and he appeared slightly out of place amongst the other pedestrians.

"Hi Tom. Are you in town to see Mary?"

"I've just come from the nursing home. She told me that you and yer mum visited her recently. That was real nice of you both. Visitors help to break up her day, and she enjoyed her chat with yer mum."

"Tom, it was our pleasure. When I told Mum about Mary, she was keen to visit and to take some magazines. We were able to wheel Mary outside into the garden, so they had quite a discussion about plants, the weather, garden pests, and then life in general, I think. It was a great change for mum too. She didn't have to focus on me for a change."

"I heard about yer little episode. No permanent damage?" He pushed the brim of his hat back, exposing his forehead, which he now massaged gently.

"Not permanently to the plane and not myself. You'll have to put up with me again shortly. I've just been cleared to return to work."

"That's good news. The mail's always nicer when you bring it, Kathy."

Settling his hat back in its original position, he continued on his way with a parting nod. Kathy watched his progress for a few moments. She had a lot or respect for Tom. He was one of a kind. She turned back to the serious business of coffee and more window shopping. At least there was some time to find the dress.

***

"So how did your flights go?"

Alex rang her in the evening, for the second day in a row. He wanted a progress report on her day, but just to hear his voice set a host of butterflies loose in her belly.

"Blitzed it of course," she said breezily. "What did you expect?"

"Nothing less, for sure. I'm glad you've got your confidence back, because I've got a job for you this weekend."

"A job? What do you mean?"

"Alice Aircraft Maintenance just called. The aircraft will be ready for pick-up at the end of the week. You can bring it out to Mulga Downs for me."

"Your plane? You want me to fly your plane out?"

"That's what I said. I need to get the plane back here, and you want to pay off some of your debt. Sounds like the perfect opportunity, doesn't it?"

His voice was silky smooth, persuasive even. Did he think she might back out on her promise? As if she had any option. Her mouth felt dry. She licked her lips, but it didn't help.

"And how will I get back to Alice? You know I'll have to work on the Monday morning."

Kathy hoped her voice didn't come across as shrill. It seemed to have risen an octave. She must remember to keep breathing. Flying was her job, and the Cessna was smaller than the aircraft she'd just flown. No problem at all.

"I can fly you back. We'll sort it out. The main thing is to get the aircraft here in the first place. You can stay the weekend. You'll be okay to do that, won't you?"

Her stomach lurched. The invitation was unexpected.

"Of course. I'll probably leave here around nine. I'll see you in time for lunch."

The call over, a hot flush of anxiety pushed Kathy out onto the veranda with a glass of cold water. She surprised herself with her reaction and was glad nobody else was around to see it. Holding the glass against her cheeks and then her forehead, she could feel the heat dissipating. What a relief.

The cicadas did their usual noisy thing. Their consistency was comforting. She hadn't changed either. She could fly that plane. Nothing to it.

Her first flight back at work was great. She was assigned a different route to her regular north-east run, and gave her the opportunity to familiarise herself with new country. Even better, she got to fly the route with Brian. She was designated navigator.

"I feel as though I've been away forever," she commented. "It's great to do something new. Anything I should specifically know about?"

"Nothing major. One of the Gardner boys has a girlfriend. That'll be interesting for Mum. Hope it doesn't make her forget the cake on our runs."

"Always thinking of your stomach. Not much has changed, then."

Kathy settled back in her seat and watched the ground sliding backwards beneath them, pencil and paper on her lap.

"This doesn't look anything like the maps I looked at last night. There are wild flowers out already. It looks like a kaleidoscopic carpet of purple and yellow. What dam is that? I should note it for future reference."

With Brian's input, she sketched her maps and made notes about the stops along the way and the people she was likely to meet. She already knew some of them. That realisation made her start to feel like a local.

Brian laughed when she mentioned it.

"A local! Don't mean to be rude, but I don't think so. I've heard that when you've seen the Todd River in flood three times, you're considered a local, but it's not quite as definable as that. There's an unspoken consensus, but I'm not sure who gets to decide."

This could be a problem. If her relationship with Alex did develop into something more permanent, would she ever be really accepted? Would she always be the outsider who pushed Melissa Gilbert aside? This was not the time to dwell on it, but as the flight progressed, the thought remained a pesky niggle at the back of her mind.

"Brian, do you consider yourself a local?"

She waited while he considered her question. They were on the final leg of their flight, having left the last stop ten minutes prior. He engaged the autopilot, and settled back, arms folded.

"Yes and no. I definitely feel part of the town, and this job has taken me all over the region. I've got to know a lot of people on the land and in the mining camps. I've been accepted, you could say, but the old families—those who've been here for generations—they wouldn't think of me as local."

He turned to look at her with a quizzical smile.

"What's this about Kathy? Does it really matter how long you've been here or what others think of you?"

Kathy pondered the question. She did her job well, and that was the most important thing. She delivered an important service and people appreciated that. She didn't have to prove herself beyond that.

"No, you're right. It doesn't matter at all. Thanks Brian. What's the name of that creek we just flew over?"

She didn't elaborate further. There were some things she wasn't ready to discuss.

When Kathy finished her flight on Friday, she made a point of dropping into the hangar workshop for Alice Aircraft Maintenance to check for herself the condition of Romeo Juliet Quebec. After introducing herself to the lead mechanic, she made a visual inspection of the aircraft, running her hands over the skin of the fuselage to check there were no ripples or other defects. Rivets could have popped on impact.

The wheel and damaged struts had been replaced and overall, the aircraft looked to be as good as new. The mechanic stood to one side, observing her assessment.

"Has it had a test flight?" It was a rhetorical question. She knew it would have happened but she felt compelled to ask.

"It has. Took off and landed beautifully. Everything has been checked and signed off as complete." If he was bemused by her questions, it didn't show. She appreciated his patience.

"And the oil pressure problem?"

"The oil pump's been replaced."

Kathy opened the cabin door and levered herself into the pilot seat. The seat was so far back, she could hardly reach the pedals. She made the necessary adjustments, and ran her eyes over the instrument panel. Everything was where it should be. The usual aircraft smell was now overlaid with a mix of lemon scent and cleaning agents. The cabin had been given the full treatment.

She sat for a while, absorbing the memories that were imbued in the aircraft frame and which seeped inside her head, a form of memory-based osmosis. She could almost hear the crumpling noise again. Repressing her anxiety, she turned on the radio. The transmissions from the Control Tower filled the cabin, crystal clear and audible. Kathy gave a sigh of relief. She knew the guys behind the microphones. She wouldn't be alone.

"And the avionics? Have they been checked?"

"Alex Woodleigh took the opportunity for everything to be tested and assessed. The radio was serviceable, but he's replaced it with the latest model. Sounds good, doesn't it?"

She climbed out of the aircraft, shutting the door carefully and walking over to where the mechanic was waiting.

"Thanks for your patience, Bruce. I'm not doubting your thoroughness. I just had to check things for myself. I'll be back in the morning to pick it up."

"I'd be surprised if you didn't want to inspect it all. See you tomorrow. I'll have it refuelled and ready to go."

Had Alex told his mother he'd invited her for the weekend? Kathy hoped so. She asked Sarah to run her out to the airport, but on the way, they dropped in at a supermarket. She couldn't go empty handed. The display of strawberries, built into a tasty pyramid caught her eye. Two punnets went into her shopping basket. Next, the weekend paper. Nothing like getting the news on time. Rounds of cheese beckoned from the display cabinet, all presenting tantalising taste options. Two of those followed, plus some cracker biscuits. A bunch of colourful gerberas completed the purchases.

Sarah looked over the selection as Kathy stashed them in the car.

"Looks like a yummy selection. I'm sure Alex will love the gerberas. Those oranges and reds are very 'him'."

"I'll tell him you said that. I thought Rose might appreciate some fresh flowers. I'll wrap some damp newspaper around the stems to help them survive the flight."

The plane had been pulled from the hangar and was waiting on the tarmac. Sarah parked in a shaded section of the car park and wandered over to watch Kathy as she shoved her bag and purchases in the luggage compartment.

"I can't believe the aircraft looks so good. Seeing her there in the sun brings back a raft of memories. You would never know what adventures she's had."

"Well, her adventurous life is over, because this is going to be a very sedate trip."

Sarah laughed at that. "I wouldn't expect anything less. I'll leave you to it. Have a good flight. Ring me when you get there."

Normally, Sarah would never make that request, but Kathy understood the reason this time. The two women embraced. Sarah walked back to the car and after completing the daily inspection, Kathy climbed aboard and with the prerequisite radio calls, was soon rolling towards the holding point. Within minutes, she was airborne.

The aircraft climbed steadily before turning onto heading and then settling into cruise level. The township disappeared, with the rooftops replaced by rolling hills and the occasional craggy gorge. The country was familiar to her, traversed many times. That was comforting. She knew where she was going.

Humming to herself, she scanned the instruments and checked the oil gauge. All indicators were as she anticipated. She could even hear the sound of her voice over the steady thrum of the engine. There was no vibration. The flight was as smooth as could be expected in a light aircraft. Try as she might, there were no inconsistencies she could see anywhere. She broke into song, the sort of song you sang when you were happy and nobody else could hear.

Reducing height as she approached Mulga Downs, she flew over the homestead before intersecting the circuit area for the strip and lining up on the final leg. It was a text-book let down, and a smooth touchdown on the gravel strip.

As she taxied back to the parking area, a Land Cruiser pulled up, a low-slung cloud of dust settling behind it. Alex swung himself from the driver's seat.

He greeted her with a kiss and a grin.

"Good flight? How did she perform?"

"She did good. We both did good. I've got a written report with me from Bruce, so you can read what he has to say but from my perspective, there are no issues at all. Love the new radio."

They pushed the aircraft into the hangar, retrieved Kathy's purchases and overnight bag, and headed back to the homestead. On the previous occasion when they drove this short distance, Kathy sat in the back, hair wet, the weather having rained on her parade. This time she sat in the front, and eagerly anticipated her time at Mulga Downs, rather than resenting the imposition.

She glanced at Alex, who had the easy driving pose of someone who was in familiar territory. He turned to look at her, their eyes meeting briefly before he looked back to the bush track unwinding before him. A hint of a smile played around his lips.

Rusty's greeting was as predictable as always. No changes there. He ran around in circles, nudged her with a wet nose and demanded her attention. Rose, who had stepped out onto the front veranda when the car pulled up, was delighted with her flowers, and welcomed Kathy with unreserved affection. Observing the interactions briefly, Alex picked up her overnight bag and the shopping, and carried them inside the house.

"You've not explored Mulga Downs, have you?"

"Well, I've seen it from the air, and then I've been to the house a couple of times, but beyond that, not really."

"Now's your chance. Come on. We can walk. Grab your hat."

Packing a broad-brimmed hat was something she'd learnt to do since coming to Alice. Kathy jammed it on her head, settling it firmly to minimise risk of it blowing off. It was slightly misshapen from being thrown around in the back of cars or planes, and being generally disrespected, but that, just added to the character.

"Where are we going?"

"Not far. Following the creek through to the gorge in the hills up behind the house. I think your mum had an exploratory visit while she was here."

"She did mention something. She was very impressed."

Rusty came too, looking at Alex defiantly as though to say, 'Don't you dare leave me behind'. He kept darting away from the track they were following, rummaging in the bushes after either real or imagined prey, before charging after them both when he thought they were getting too far ahead.

The track was narrow, sometimes following a smooth, well-trodden path and sometimes becoming an obstacle course of ancient rocks, leading the way further into the cleft in the hills. The creek was dry in places, the tidemarks against the banks indicating where water had once been. In other sections, there were small stagnant rock pools, surrounded by water reeds and dive-bombed by various winged insects. The further they walked, the wider the pools became until the isolated puddles linked together and became a meandering channel.

When the track was wide enough, they walked side by side, sometimes brushing against each other as they negotiated the uneven ground. Only a short time ago, such contact on the back of her hand would have caused Kathy to recoil, the electrical charge being a discordant shock. Now the contact was more likely to attract rather than repel.

"See this?" Alex drew her attention to a bloodwood tree. He pointed to the knobbly fruit, lying on the ground close underneath.

"Here you have the bush coconut. The flesh inside is edible. So are the grubs that have sometimes burrowed in. Want to try?"

"No thanks. I've just had lunch. But you feel free."

He laughed. "Nothing wrong with dessert."

She noted he didn't follow up on his own suggestion. He also pointed out the little grass wrens and to her surprise, a flock of budgerigars.

"I don't think I've ever seen them outside of a cage. This is a much better environment. Aren't they beautiful, but so noisy!"

The temperature dropped as they neared the pool at the base of the gorge. Footprints at the edge of the water indicated they were not the only visitors.

"There are quite a few rock wallabies around here, but there might be the odd kangaroo, dingo and other beast as well. It's a permanent waterhole, and that'll be local knowledge."

There was a large flat-topped rock by the water's edge, and they sat for a while, just looking and absorbing the atmosphere. There was a distinct metallic smell in the air, and the surrounding trees cast long shadows. Rusty dropped to a panting rest on the sand.

"Mulga Downs is more than just cattle," Alex said after a while. "It's centuries of history, mixed up with all the natural wonders the ranges offer. We're privileged to live here. I wouldn't live in the city for quids."

"There are lots of benefits of living in a city as well," Kathy swiped at a flying insect that came too close. "There's opportunity, beaches, cultural events, restaurants, family and friends…"

She threw her arms wide expansively to demonstrate the scope of the city.

"And don't we have all of that here? It's just in a more regionally distinctive form. We might not have the beaches," he said, the glint in his eye more suggestive than his words, "but I do know some wonderful places to swim."

Kathy dragged her gaze from watching the dive-bombing insects to look at him appraisingly.

"So, there are more you can show me?" Her voice was coquettish, teasing even.

"There are, but that will take some time."

"I'll have to stick around a little longer then, won't I?"

His answer was without words. Reaching for her, he claimed her lips with a passion that left her breathless and aching for more. She wasn't going anywhere in a hurry.

***

Kathy carefully laid the dress on top of the rest of her luggage. She had used tissue inserts in the folds, and wrapped a final layer of tissue around the garment. She surveyed the contents of the bag one last time before zipping it closed.

There was always that nagging feeling that something had been left behind. She would just have to deal with that.

She heard the car pull up outside followed by footsteps coming towards the flat. Alex stood framed in the doorway. Her heart still did a little jump each time she saw him there.

"All packed and ready?" he asked.

"I've got all I need, and if I've forgotten anything, I'll just have to buy a replacement in Adelaide. I'll probably do some shopping, anyway. Any requests?

"Just don't stay away too long. There's still a lot of work you can do on Mulga Downs."

Her eyebrows arched. "Is that all you care about? You've got a strange way of wooing a girl. No wonder you've been on your own so long!"

He leant forward to kiss her cheek and picked up her bag.

"You'd better get in the car before I show you a more interactive way of wooing a girl."

She chuckled as she followed him outside, locking the door behind her. "Promises, promises."

The drive to the airport took them out through Heavitree Gap, the entrance to the town for the Todd River and the Ghan train service. The river bed, dry except for isolated pools, meandered beside the tracks for a while before veering off, the tall gums marking its progress.

Kathy looked at it with the eyes she'd had when the train had rolled into Alice. It had seemed so alien then. Now, it seemed like home.

She glanced over at Alex.

"I'm looking forward to catching up with everyone, and of course attending Jessie's wedding. I never thought I would say this, but I'll be looking forward to coming back to Alice as well."

"Just to Alice?"

"Now you're fishing!"

The carpark at the airport was crowded, with aircraft arrivals and departures focussed on the middle of the day. Alex found a vacant bay towards the rear, just beating a Holden to the spot, with a cheery wave to the driver. Parking conflicts were rare in Alice!

Kathy stepped out of the car and stretched, easing some cricks from her back before bending to pick up her suitcase.

"I'll take that."

Alex pushed her gently out the way and grabbed the suitcase, leaving his other hand free to hold hers as they walked towards the airport terminal. It wasn't quite as crowded as the railway platform had been, but the comparisons were stark in her memory. Who knew then how the future was going to unfold?

With check-in formalities complete, boarding calls were made and she had to leave. Passengers lined up at the exit gate. Kathy turned to him.

"My flight's being called."

With all the anticipation of the trip, she hadn't expected to feel like this. She was looking forward to the vibrancy of the city, and the wedding and her family and everything she had missed, but part of her didn't want to go. Her smile was hesitant.

He leaned forward and kissed her. "Enjoy yourself, sweetheart. Call me."

Throwing him one last wordless look, she turned and headed for the gate. This time, the plane was in the competent hands of someone else, and she could sit back and enjoy the ride. Walking across the tarmac, Kathy paused, avoiding the passengers walking behind her and looked back towards the terminal building. She could see the figure of a tall man, wearing moleskins and boots, hands on hips, outlined at the window. Waving, she could swear that those grey eyes connected with hers.

There was a brief nod of acknowledgement. She turned and climbed the steps to the plane. In her heart she knew there would be a time when she didn't travel alone. There would be a tall bushman by her side, someone who welcomed her into his life and shared hers. There might be yet another wedding in her future.

The End

If you enjoyed this book, please leave a review where you purchased it, or on Goodreads or Bookbub.

'**Trust Your Heart**', the second book in the Red Centre Series, follows Sarah's story as she navigates life following the death of her fiancé. Order it from my website, www.emilyhussey.com.au.

Australia

The Red Heart is set in Alice Springs, which is in the centre of Australia and the southern-most city of the Northern Territory. Kathy's family lives in Adelaide, the capital city of South Australia.

FIVE MINUTES OF YOUR TIME

I'd love to hear your thoughts after reading *The Red Heart*. There are several ways you can do that:

- emailing me at emily@emilyhussey.com.au
- posting on Facebook at https://www.facebook.com/EmilyHusseyAuthor/
- Leaving a review on the website from which you purchased the book

Your comments will help me in delivering a great story, and your reviews will be helpful to future readers.

Thank you

Emily Hussey

THE RED CENTRE SERIES

The **Red Centre Series** is set in and around Alice Springs, in the centre of Australia and also known as the Red Centre. Meet all the central characters in the prequel, **Journey to the Heart**.

~

The Red Heart

Kathy Sullivan is excited about taking up her new job as a pilot in Alice Springs. She was surprised at the antagonism directed towards her by Alex Woodleigh, owner of Mulga Downs. She knew that it could be hot in the Red Centre, but Kathy had no idea how much heat she would generate. In the sky, she was in full command, but back on the ground she was in danger of losing her cool. Emotions peak when disaster strikes during a remote flight, forcing them to acknowledge the underlying cause of their conflict and antagonism.

Trust Your Heart

Embracing liquid refreshments a little more exuberantly than usual, Sarah falls off a table and into Joel's life. She introduces him to life in and around Alice Springs, but secrecy, for whatever reasons, gives rise to more problems than it hides. As water rises around him in the flooding Todd River, Joel is forced to question who he trusts. Is it too late for him to convince Sarah that with him, she has a chance for renewed happiness?

Emily Hussey

Follow Your Heart

Tragic events in her formative years colour Melissa's perceptions of her place in the world. Trust and commitment are not concepts she embraces. In a journey that takes her from a remote Australian station, to the high fashion world of Sydney and beyond, Melissa learns valuable lessons. She realises that family can be broader than you appreciate, and that she has choices to make in who she lets into her life, and who she loves.

Don't miss out on your free download!

If you enjoyed this story, you might like to read a collection of short stories in

Romance in the Stone

To receive your *free* copy, and keep up-to-date with news about future releases,

copy and paste https://bit.ly/3qQdbqR into your browser.

ABOUT THE AUTHOR

Emily Hussey has lived in several Australian states, and that experience has provided useful backdrop for some of her novels. She spent her twenties in Alice Springs, which became the setting for the Red Centre Series. She now resides on the coast in the city of Adelaide, and is exploring the writing options in every café in walking distance.

Emily was a marriage celebrant for 24 years, and has married couples in many different locations, ranging from private gardens, to beaches, to caves, or rural locations. Many of her clients remain friends to this day. She usually writes with Iris, a black and white cat at her elbow, demanding her share of attention. Writing tends to be fuelled with regular coffee boosts, and occasional squares of very dark chocolate.